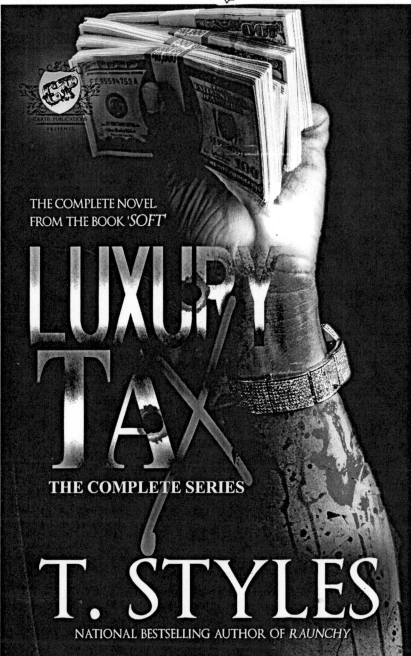

THE COMPLETE NOVEL
FROM THE BOOK '*SOFT*'

LUXURY TAX

THE COMPLETE SERIES

T. STYLES

NATIONAL BESTSELLING AUTHOR OF *RAUNCHY*

Library of Congress Control Number: 2013947405
ISBN 10: 098908454X

ISBN 13: 9780989084543

Cover Design: Davida Baldwin www.oddballdsgn.com
Graphics: Davida Baldwin
www.thecartelpublications.com
First Edition

Printed in the United States of America

ARE YOU ON

OUR EMAIL

LIST?

SIGN UP ON OUR WEBSITE
www.thecartelpublications.com
OR TEXT THE WORD: CARTELBOOKS TO
22828
FOR PRIZES, CONTESTS, ETC.

CHECK OUT OTHER TITLES BY THE CARTEL PUBLICATIONS

WWW.THECARTELPUBLICATIONS.COM

What's Up Fam,

With no delay, I'ma jump directly into the novel at hand, "Luxury Tax." The first part of this story was released in an anthology called, **"Soft: Cocaine Love Stories"**. T. Styles' contribution, "Luxury Tax" was so good, fans called for more and she delivered. You will love how this story plays out and how part two (eBook version) picks up right where the first one left off. Here's a hint, look out for characters who make a cameo in this novel that have been in T. Styles' other tales to see how good you are.

Keeping in line with tradition, we want to give respect to a trailblazer paving the way. With that said we would like to recognize:

Robert McKee is the author of, "Story: Substance, Structure, Style and The Principles of Screenwriting". Mr. McKee does a great job of breaking down scenes and chapters to help you excel in telling your story. Although this is a book about screenwriting, his teachings also apply to penning novels as well. If this is something you are interested in or are looking to sharpen your skills on, check this author and novel out.

Ok, go 'head and dive in! I'll holla at you in the next novel.

Be Easy!
Charisse "C. Wash" Washington
Vice President
The Cartel Publications
www.thecartelpublications.com
www.twitter.com/cartelbooks
www.facebook.com/cartelpublications

Dedication

I dedicate this novel to all my fans. I love you.

"...there's a luxury tax when you fuck with rich niggas. You don't get to floss without a price. And it's time you recognize that shit."
-Nicky

CHAPTER 1

GINGER
BACK IT UP

Kentland, Maryland was hot as shit the day Trixy Greggs stepped her funky ass up to me. I was sitting in front of Carmen and her sister's house smoking a blunt when she walked up with some bullshit. You'd never know it, but six months ago, we were cool. That is until I bumped my head after returning home from vacation one night, which resulted in my memory loss. When I came to, my best friend was missing, people were mad at me and my boyfriend Milli was acting different.

"That's fucked up what you did to Quita!" She said, sweat pouring down her face causing her makeup to streak. "Just 'cause she spanked your daughter for pissing on herself."

"Bitch, that's between me and Quita and you ain't got shit to do with it."

"What you gonna do? Slice my throat too?" She taunted.

"If that's what you want!" She took a step closer and I said, "Trixy, I'm warning you...step outta my face."

She laughed and said, "...and what kind of mother are you? If my baby was taken by Child Protective Services, I'd be trying to get her back, not outside running my mouth like you."

"Bitch, get your rotten pussy ass outta my face."

"Come on, Trixy," her best friend Shonda said pulling her arm. "This bitch ain't worth it."

"Fuck that," she said shaking Shonda off with one body shiver. "I wonder if Milli feel the same way about me as you do, Ginger." She smirked.

Bitches loved saying Milli's name outta they mouths. He ran Kentland and every bitch in Kentland wanted him but he chose me. One of these days these washed up hoes was going to realize it.

"What you trying to say, Trixy?" My True Religion jeans were damp because I was sweating so much.

"Come, on Trix," Shonda interrupted again, her light skin flushed. "You don't want shit to go too far out here." The look on their faces told me they knew something I didn't.

"Why don't you just move the fuck from around here?" Trixy asked me. "Don't nobody even fuck with you no more!"

"I wanna know what you meant by saying Milli's name outta your mouth," I said ready to drop her ass.

She laughed and said, "All I know is you betta not kiss him any time soon on them sexy ass lips of his."

6

I snapped. When I came to, half of the cheap ass weave she had in her head was on the ground by my feet, and she had bald spots in places her hair should've been. I had beaten the brakes off of her ass in a pair of black Dior heels and I wasn't done.

"You think I did something now, you betta be glad my Benz wasn't parked on the curb. I got shit in my trunk for bitches like you!"

I saw my friend Nicky push through the crowd to get at me. "Come on, Ginger, we gotta go now!" She pulled my arm and the police sirens grew louder. They were close.

"You ain't did shit but make me mad," Trixy said. "And before the night is over, you gonna see me again."

"Bitch, take your bald headed ass in the house and look in the mirror! I did more than just make you mad!"

Trixy was right about one thing, after that shit she just pulled, she was definitely gonna see me again.

Nicky and me were on the way to my house when about fifteen kids blocked our path. Five of them belonged to Nicky's cousin Stevie, and they all looked dirty and nasty, but seventeen-year old Crystal's fresh ass was the worst of them all. I couldn't stand that little bitch and I think she knew it too. I caught her sitting on my car one day and asked her to get off. She rolled her eyes and later that day, I saw scratches on my paint job. She was just like her mother...a little whore in the making.

"Hey, aunt Nicky, you know where mama at?" She asked resting her hand on her hips. This little girl was too grown.

She was talking to Nicky but looking at me. "I like your shoes, Ginger."

"Thanks," I said nonchalantly.

Everything I wore was of a designer brand, including the Fendi shades I propped in my shoulder length hair, and the white Armani t-shirt clinging to my back.

Crystal's younger sister Melissa, who I believed was slightly retarded, stood next to her. She never said much outside of hi and bye.

"I want some sunflower seeds and a pickled sausage," Melissa said outta nowhere.

"Shut up and wait," Crystal said yanking her arm. "Aunt Nicky, we hungry and can't find ma. You know where she at."

"Well she ain't with me. When I see her I'ma give her your message," she said pushing past them.

Crystal stomped away yanking her sister by the arm.

"That's sad Stevie ain't get Melissa no help yet," I said to Nicky. "She acts like she retarded."

"She ain't retarded!" She laughed. "Just slow."

"Ya'll keep thinking that shit if you want to, but something's wrong with that lil' girl."

When I turned around I saw Melissa looking at me. I think she heard what I said. Oh well, I was too hot and mad to give a fuck if she heard me or not. I just had my third fight for the week and Milli was getting tired of my shit.

"Why you and Trixy beefing anyway?" Nicky asked.

"I wish I knew. I know if she don't keep Milli's name outta her mouth, I'ma put something to her ass that's going to lay her down for good, Nicky. I'm all the way serious 'bout that shit."

"You ain't got to tell me," she laughed, "Everybody in the neighborhood know you got a temper." I placed my shades on my eyes. "She ask you if you remember again?" she asked.

"She ain't ask me, but I'm sick of people not believing I don't remember shit. What I gotta lie for? If anything I feel like people keeping shit from me 'round here. Nobody understands what it's like to lose your memory, only to wake up and have your best friend missing, and your world changed. You heard anything about Leona?"

"Naw, but you know I'd tell you if I did," she said searching my eyes.

"Shit just don't feel right," I said. "I feel like me falling and Leona being missing connects some how. It doesn't help that her parents think I had something to do with it."

"Ginger, I don't know about her parents, but people around here are upset. It's been six months and the police be around here every other day asking questions about Leona. And her father being a police officer makes shit worse. You ever thought about moving?"

"What, and leave Milli around this hoe spot by himself?"

"Take him with you."

"He don't wanna move even though we don't *really* live together anyway. Plus he make too much money over here," I swallow hard because I want to ask her something I really don't want to know the answer to. "You think Milli cheating?"

We stopped walking and she said, "Ginger, there's a luxury tax when you fuck with rich niggas. You don't get to floss without a price. And it's time you recognize that shit."

"I hear you, but there's a luxury tax when you fuck with a bad bitch too, Nicky. It ain't like I can't get another man to do for me what Milli does."

"Can you? And if you could why would you want to? All rich niggas cheat, Ginger. It's their right. Just one bitch ain't enough no more."

She just said some bullshit but I said, "So you saying he *is* cheating on me?"

"I think he's a nigga and niggas gonna do nigga shit."

"Nigga shit or not, if I find out he's fucking around on me, I'll cut his ass off quick. And he betta hope that's just it. You know I can be violent when I want to."

"That's on you but it wouldn't be me losing him. Look at your arm. How many bitches you know with a four-carat diamond bracelet? You should let some shit pass, Ginger."

She was referring to the diamond bracelet Milli got me when we first got together. I cherished this bracelet; because it was the first thing he ever bought me.

Nicky knew a lot about rich niggas cause hustler's loved her. She let 'em do what they wanted as long as the money flowed like a fountain. A little shorter than me at five foot four, she had a big personality and big ass titties too. It didn't hurt that she was a cute red-bone.

"I know you twenty-six years old...one year older than me, but you talk old as shit sometimes," I said laughing.

"I just know niggas. But to answer your question, I don't think he fucking Trixy dusty ass. The bitch too nasty."

Maybe that's why she let her cousin Stevie fuck her ex-boyfriend Raheem, who she was with for two years, and get away with it. Nicky was all about the money and nothing else mattered, not even love.

"Now if you want somebody else to have him then let him go," she continued. "He wouldn't be on the market long I can tell you that much."

I wish I would see another bitch with Milli. That nigga had me in a new Benz every six months. His name wasn't Milli for nothing! At twenty-six he was already a self-made millionaire.

"Come on, Nick...that ain't even in the talk."

"Well then drop that shit and focus on getting your daughter back instead. When you gotta go to court for slicing Quita anyway?"

11

"Next week."

"Umph, well...I would steer clear of trouble if I were you. Let me go in the house real quick. I'm coming back later to hit a jay with you," she said running up the street.

When I walked up the steps in front of my house, I tensed up when I saw the dark brown blood stain on my step. It's the place where I fell and lost my memory and no matter how hard I scrubbed, it never went away. And no matter how hard I wished my memory of that night would return, it never did.

Once inside my house, I was lonely. Lately Milli ain't been the same and I miss him. What's the use of having money if you alone all the time? If you don't have a nigga there to hold you?

I locked the front door and grabbed the trash bag in the kitchen to put it out back. The moment I opened my back door I saw Gerron, my next-door neighbor doing push-ups in his backyard. Sweat poured from his body and his muscles buckled under the hot summer sun.

It didn't help that he was so damn sexy. Who works out in no shirt and a pair of jeans and still look so good? He looked like Columbus Short from the movie *Stomp the Yard*, but a few years older. He had the same full lips and smooth caramel skin and body.

We had a funny kinda relationship. I use to be able to talk to him about anything, but after I fell and lost my memory, even he treated me differently. I went over his house a couple of times to talk to him, to ask if he remembered anything about that night, but he kept saying he didn't know nothing. I think he was lying.

I took the lid off the can and acted like I didn't see him when he said, "You up there fighting them clucking bitches again?" He stopped doing his sets and stood up. "Why you keep dealing with them ratchet chickens?"

"You talking to me?" I pointed to myself.

"I never stopped talking to you. I just ain't wanna talk 'bout what you wanted to talk about."

"How you hear 'bout the fight already anyway? The shit just happened."

"I know everything."

And then he looked at me, with those eyes. The eyes that almost get me in trouble whenever I'm around him.

"Stop looking at me like that," I said.

"Why? You finally admitting you want a nigga or something?"

"Not even...we could never take it there 'cause I have a boyfriend and you a stick-up nigga."

"Come on, Ginger," he said patting his face with a white towel. "First off you don't know what I do to earn my paper." He breathed heavily. "You going off what these muthafuckas 'round here say. Have I ever hit that rich ass nigga you with before?"

"Naw."

"Aight then. A stick-up nigga would not have passed up on the opportunity to get that payday." He smiled slyly. "Now come on over here so I can taste that pussy of yours."

My heart jumped. He never talked to me like that and it made me wonder why. Part of me was angry but the other part was turned on.

"Oh so what...now you gonna disrespect me?"

"That's disrespecting you, by asking can I taste your pussy? I mean what's wrong with it?"

"What...what you think?"

He laughed and said, "Yeah, aight. If you so disrespected why you still out here?"

"Boy, this my house and I do what I want to."

He laughed. "Look...bottom line, you with a nigga who could care less about you. Yet you push away a nigga that's been feeling you from day one. But you gonna need me one day." Then he put the gun that was sitting on his step in his waist and threw his white t-shirt over his shoulder. "I just hope it ain't too late."

I hate his ass! Don't get it twisted, Gerron was sexy but not sexier than Milli. Milli's six foot two inch frame floated over my five foot six inch frame just like I liked it. Plus Milli could afford me and Gerron's money was too 'iffy'. You could make but so much, robbing other niggas.

When I went into the house, I got a bottle of water and decided to call Milli since I hadn't spoken to him all day. So I grabbed my cell outta my Gucci purse.

"What it do, babes?" he asked answering the phone after the third ring. His voice was raspy and sexy as usual.

"Nothing, but I can't wait to see you tonight."

"Why you sound like you stressing? That cop been 'round the way again asking 'bout Leona?"

"Naw, not today." I sat on the couch and flipped my shoes off to rub my sore feet. The air from the open window cooled me off a little. When I saw my hands were red with blood from beating Trixy's fat ass, I went into the kitchen to wash them.

"Let me send you on that vacation we talked about."

I walked back into the living room and sat on the sofa. "I don't wanna leave if you not going with me."

"I told you I can't get away right now, but I still want you to enjoy yourself. Shit, take Nicky with you if you want."

"Maybe," I said not feeling like being stuck with her for a whole week. I think he wanted me gone for a while too because the cops were hassling me. But if I left, what's to say the cops would leave the neighborhood? Leona still is missing.

"Man, just let me know when you ready," he continued. "And why you ain't answer your phone when I hit you earlier?"

"The house phone?"

"Yeah. I told you I was gonna call you back."

"Oh...uh...I was up the street," I responded.

"What you doing up there?" He said as if he knew I was in another fight.

"Talking to Carmen. They invited me to a party."

"Oh...they ain't still talking 'bout the fall are they? I'm tired of niggas getting in your business."

"Nobody really in my business."

"You know I'm digging all the way in that pussy when I see you right? You been playing with yourself lately?"

"Yeah, but I want you to do it for me, Milli." I figure I might as well tell him about the fight since he's in a good mood thinking about my pussy. If there was one thing he loved to do, fucking was it. I caught him several times jacking off and believed he had a sex addiction. "Baby...I fought Trixy today."

"What the fuck happen this time?" he sighed.

"She said some shit I ain't like."

"Why you can't walk away from the ordinary and step up when necessary? You acting young and dumb...always believing these bitches when they tell you I fucked them. Your temper's outta control, Ginger. You gotta get that shit right. It's gonna get you in a lot of trouble one day if you don't."

I was just getting ready to plead my case when someone threw a bottle with fire through my window. When it hit my hardwood floor it broke and flames spread everywhere. I threw water on it and smothered the rest with one of the couch pillows. Then I ran to my front door, opened it up only to see some skinny bitch with black shorts running up the street barefoot. She's one of Trixy's friends and I couldn't wait to catch up with that bitch later.

"Ginger! What the fuck is up?" I heard Milli yell.

"Tell Trixy her ass is as good as dead," I screamed out of the window.

I was so mad I didn't care if Milli was on the phone or not, but now I had to deal with him. I put the phone to my ear.

"What the fuck is going on, Ginger?"

"Some hating ass bitch just threw fire through the window! I'm cool though."

I looked at the shattered glass on my living room floor and flopped down on the sofa.

"I heard you scream. You 'aight?" Gerron asked coming through my back door while I was on the phone with Milli.

I put my hand over my cell and whispered, "Yeah...but Milli's on the phone. You gotta go."

He frowned and walked out.

"Ginger, maybe you should move," Milli said to me on the phone. "Shit getting serious 'round there."

"I'm not letting no dumb ass bitches run me from outta my house, Milli."

"Who you talking to baby?" I heard a woman say in the background on the phone.

Click.

"Hello?"

He hung up the phone. What the fuck? I called Milli back four times and each call went to his voicemail. I'm so mad I feel like fighting again. He waited five minutes before calling me back.

"Milli, what's up? Who was that bitch in the background?"

"Nobody, Tracy over here playing too much."

My cell phone beeped because my battery was running low, and I wanted to say I'd call him on my house phone, but I needed to know the truth first. I didn't want to risk the chance of him not answering if I switched phones.

"Your cousin?"

"Yeah…who the fuck you think I'm talking 'bout?"

I don't believe him and for the first time ever I test his loyalty. "Milli, put her on the phone."

Although I've never met Tracey because she doesn't like me and I don't like her, I know her voice when I hear it. And that's only because whenever she watches my daughter, I always call to check on her.

"So you don't trust me?" He asked with an attitude. "That's what you saying?"

Normally I'd back down but this time I'm standing my ground. "I wanna talk to her."

A few seconds later Tracey got on the phone and said, "What the fuck you want with me, bitch?"

It was her.

A second later, Milli returned to the phone and said, "You gonna wish you never doubted me, Ginger."

Click.

What the fuck was I thinking? If Milli cut me off how was I gonna take care of myself? I put my shoes back on and stood up. Glass was everywhere and it crushed under my feet. I plugged my cell phone up to the charger and decided to call him back on my house phone, but when I picked-up the handset, someone was on the line.

"Milli, is this you?" I asked whoever was on the phone.

"H...hello. Can Renee talk on the phone please?" A little girl asked me.

For the past two weeks, this little bitch got my number mixed up with Shonda's next door, and every time she did it got on my fucking nerves. If I spoke to Shonda cordially I would have told her to set her ass straight. But I didn't like Shonda and she didn't like me so we never said a word to one another.

"How many times I gotta tell you, you calling the wrong number?"

"I'm sorry," she said softly.

"Don't be sorry, just stop fucking calling my house!" I slammed the phone down and rubbed my aching forehead.

After I hung up, I called Nicky because I needed somebody to talk to. She probably gonna give me that luxury tax bullshit again, but she's all I got since Leona left. I miss Leona's friendship so much it burns my chest sometimes. She was so good with things like this.

When Nicky finally answered I said, "When you coming back over?"

"Fifteen minutes why?"

"Hurry up, I'm blown and I need to hit that jay."

"I'm getting dressed now, girl. Rico just stopped by and we beefing so give me about twenty minutes," she said referring to her boyfriend.

"Aight…and I'ma tell you 'bout the fire somebody threw in my window when you get here."

"See, this what the fuck I'm talking 'bout. Every time I come over here, your ass is on the fucking phone. This why our relationship ain't working. Everybody else more important than me," Rico said in the background, sounding like a stone cold bitch.

"Girl go ahead and care for your nigga," I said. "I'll talk to you later. But before you leave, can you grab the money you owe me too? Milli and me beefing and he might cut me off like he usually does when he's mad. I need to build back up my stash."

"Yeah, I'll ask Rico for it," she said with a slightly different attitude. I hate when people made you feel bad for asking for your money back. "Me and Stevie will be over in a minute." She hung up.

Damn I wish she'd just leave Stevie's ass home so I can talk to her alone. Who hangs out with somebody who fucked their man anyway? Cousin or not? When I hung up with her, I prepped the rest of my dinner for the night. Through my window I could see the back of Gerron's house and I started to walk over there to talk to him, but knew that would turn into something else. Like me fucking him which I never did.

Instead I swept the glass up from my floor and made me a glass of Bacardi Limon straight up. I had to refill my glass four times to clear my mind. After that I turned my stereo on and Usher's *"Love You Gently"* song blasted from the speakers so I put on Lil Wayne's Carter 3 CD instead. I didn't feel like hearing the romantic shit right now. I decided to wait outside on the porch for Nicky but hoped I'd see the bitch that threw something in my house too. I swear these bitches won't be satisfied until I killed somebody.

I was looking at a group of kids fighting each other when my phone rang again. I ran into the house, grabbed it and walked back outside.

"Hello," I said hoping it was Milli. I miss him already.

"Can Renee talk on the phone?"

I frowned and was immediately annoyed. I sat on the porch. "Why you keep calling my house?" I sighed.

"I keep getting the number mixed up. I'm sorry."

"How come I don't believe you?" I asked her.

Silence.

"What's your name?" I continued.

"Rhianna." I laughed knowing immediately that she was lying. "Are you busy, Ginger?"

I thought it was weird that she knew my name, but figured if she caught my voicemail from when I didn't answer the phone, she could've gotten it from there.

"So now you wanna talk to me instead of Renee?"

"Yes."

"And what do you want to talk to me about?"

"I wanted to tell you that I heard my mommy say that some man in a red car is gonna set your friend Nicky up."

My heart dropped. "Fuck you talking 'bout set her up?"

"My mommy be playing Spades with her friends and I heard them say that yesterday."

"Who's your mother?" I stood up. "'Cause if you knew me you wouldn't be pulling no bullshit like this!"

Click.

"Hello! Hello!" I screamed into the handset.

I sat on the porch again.

"Who you yelling at now, girl?" Nicky asked walking up to me. She sat on the step beside me and her cousin Stevie sat a few steps down from us, as she sang along with the music in my house.

I put the phone down trying to decide if I should tell her about the call or not.

"Ain't nobody girl...they must've h...had the wrong number," I stuttered.

Nicky was wearing a cute Gucci green tank top and a pair of Bvlgari shades. "Here's the money I borrowed from you last week," Nicky said handing me my cash. She would probably borrow it back before the week was out if me and Milli got back together. I only needed it now because I don't know what Milli was going to do.

Stevie looked at the money Nicky handed me and I saw a twinge of jealousy in her eyes. Nicky gave me a lot of twenties, even though I gave her one hundreds when she borrowed it, but it was cool. I tucked all three grand in my pocket.

The moment I sat down, I saw an unmarked police car pull up. He might as well've drove a marked car because we'd seen officer Harvey Chance so many times 'round here, we could smell him from miles away.

"How you doing this evening ladies?" he asked as he approached us. He wore a designer pair of black slacks and a black shirt. His Black and grey Fendi glasses sat comfortably on the bridge of his nose.

Although he irritated the fuck out of me, he was still very attractive for an older man.

"Ms. Spellman, have you heard anything about Leona Claremont?"

"I already told ya'll I ain't hear shit and don't know shit. She was my friend, why wouldn't I tell ya'll if I knew something?"

I saw a few people looking at me talking to him, and I hated that this was the main reason my neighborhood wanted me gone. With the cops coming around all the time asking me questions, it made it hard to sell drugs and customers were going to other blocks to cop.

"We don't know, but it seems unnatural that she'd disappear off the face of the earth without anybody knowing anything. You were the last person she called and she hasn't been seen or heard from since."

"Well like I told ya'll before, I was out of town when she called me, and ya'll already checked the cell records so you know I'm telling the truth."

He looked at me, Nicky and then Stevie. "Well, I'll be in touch again." He walked toward his car.

Sometimes I think he asked me the same questions just to see me go the fuck off. A few of my neighbors shook their heads at me and walked back into their houses. I thought it was kinda funny that they were mad at me because they couldn't do illegal shit because of the cops being around here all of the time. I mean really, get a fucking job!

When Officer Chance got in his car and waved, I threw the "fuck you" sign in the air at him.

"You talk to Milli about the fight with Trixy yet?" Nicky asked looking at the cop drive out of sight.

"Yeah...but that window shit got me fucked up now."

Nicky stood up, dusted the dirt off her ass and looked in my front window at the burn on the floor. She sat back down on the step and said, "I don't see how you stay around here. Unless they find Leona, shit like this is not going to stop happening."

"So maybe they'll find her."

"Yeah right," she laughed looking at Stevie.

That hurt. I wanted nothing more than to see my friend's face again.

"I mean really, Ginger, what's so good about Kentland anyway? Why not just move?"

"It's the principle plus I ain't do shit to move."

"I heard some bitches up the street say they gonna step to you again, Ginger," Stevie added with a smirk on her face. She loved that I was having bad days, I knew it. "You don't want 'em fucking with your car next do you?"

"Who said that shit?" I asked.

"I ain't getting in it. I'm just letting you know 'cause we cool."

I was thinking, '*why even say something, bitch*', when Crystal spotted her mother at my house and ran up to us. A rack of kids followed her. The moment they got into my space, I could smell the sweat and dirt from their skin and wanted to throw up.

"Ma, can I have a five dooooollllaaaas?" Crystal asked dragging her words.

What the fuck is A five dooooollllasss?

"What you 'bout to buy?"

"A hot sausage and some nacho cheese sunflower seeds."

"Bring me some seeds back too," Stevie said reaching into her pocket, just like she did whenever she *pretended* to have money. When her hands came out empty, she patted her pockets as if some would magically appear. "You got any money on you, Nicky? I'll give it back to you when I get my check on the first."

"I ain't got shit but a C-note. I just gave Ginger all my money," She said looking at me.

*No bitch, you just gave me all *my* money. I thought.*

"Please, Miss Ginger," Crystal whined, with the other kids chiming in too.

I started to tell them broke ass bitches to get the fuck off my steps, instead I dug into my pockets and pulled out twenty dollars. I handed the bill to Crystal and said, "Buy everybody something."

She snatched the money out of my hands and ran. Do you know this nasty bitch ain't even say thank you, and her mother didn't make her either?

"She said buy us all something," one of the boys reminded Crystal as they ran down the street. *"It ain't just for you."*

"You bring the jay?" I asked shaking my head at the foolishness I just witnessed.

"Naw, a friend of mine on his way to see me. He usually got smoke too."

"I thought you had one rolled up already?"

"I did, but somebody decided to help themselves to my shit when I wasn't looking," she said looking at Stevie rolling her eyes.

"Shit, you was taking all day," Stevie responded. "So I fired up."

"Fuck that shit, Stevie," Nicky said. "I was looking forward to blazing. Now you got us out here on the natural."

"I told you I got money on the next pack," she lied. She never had money on shit, not even on her bills.

"You ain't even have money to give your kids," Nicky said, saying what I was thinking.

My attention was briefly taken off her, and put on the group of girls who walked by my house. They hang with Trixy, the bitch I was beefing with.

"Is it hot in there?" one of the girls asked. "I heard your place was on fire."

"Bitch, what you say?" I yelled standing up.

"Take that shit down the street," Nicky jumped in. "Ya'll don't want to see Ginger go off out here, 'cause can't none of ya'll fuck with her wreck game."

They all looked at me, laughed and walked away. I was contemplating running up to them but my phone rang again. I didn't want to answer it because that girl had me shook. But what if it was Milli?

"Hello."

"Is Ginger Spellman available?"

"Bitch, you called my house, who the fuck is this?"

"Ms. Spellman, this is Lucy Cunningham from the office of Child Protective services. Is now a bad time to speak with you?"

I stood up straight, threw on my professional voice and said, "Oh...uh... no. I thought you were somebody playing on my phone. I can talk now."

"I see...well can you turn the music down in the background a little? I can barely hear you."

I rushed inside the house, turned the music down and stood inside in front of the glass door.

"That's better," she said. "I'm calling about Denise Knox. Is she your daughter?"

"Yes, ma'am."

"Well I'm calling to tell you that we have detected crack cocaine in her system."

"Fuck you talking 'bout?"

"Like I said, crack is in the child's system. We tested her because she was exhibiting behavior fitting of a child who has been exposed to drugs. She wets the bed frequently, her behavior is irrational—"

"She's a child," I interrupted.

"Ma'am, we've seen enough children to know the symptoms. Therefore we have scheduled an appointment with you on Monday of next week. We have to discuss this matter."

"Ma'am, there's been a mistake. I don't even know anybody on crack."

"We'll see about that when we meet you. You'll also have to submit to testing yourself."

There was no use reasoning with this bitch so I said, "Okay, but where is she right now? I been calling all over but nobody seems to know nothing."

"I'll get to that in a minute, ma'am," she paused. "*Now*...we need you to bring us proof of employment when you come so that we can make an evaluation on Denise's placement, that is, in the event things work out for you in criminal court. You are facing very serious charges."

This bitch made my blood boil. "I got all that, but can you tell me where they have my baby?"

"She's with," she paused as I heard the sound of papers shuffle in the background, "let's see...she's at Terrod Knox's cousin's house. Her name is Tracey Knox. Terrod is the child's father right?"

Terrod Knox is Milli.

"Yeah, when did she get there?" I asked confused. "And why couldn't she stay with my mother like I asked?"

"Because your mother works two jobs and is unable to care for her. The only other alternative is foster care, and I know you don't want that. So she was sent to Tracey's house about an hour ago."

Milli probably didn't know where she was when I spoke to him earlier because he didn't say anything to me. I was just happy she was with family even if it was Tracey.

"Now if everything is in order, after my evaluation, she can be back in your care, before no time. Just remember to bring the documentation that I asked for. We also have to pray things work out in court."

"Okay. I should be able to do that."

"By the way, how *are* you supporting yourself?"

"I have a job."

"Well it's imperative that you bring that verification of your job from your employer. You must understand, Ms. Spellman, the kind of violence you exhibited in front of those children at the daycare center was very serious. It's a wonder you're not still in jail. The child care provider could have died."

"…That dumb bitch Quita hit my, baby," I blurted out, causing Nicky and Stevie to look back at me. "I don't play that shit!"

Silence.

"Ms. Spellman, I'm going to also recommend that you attend anger management classes. Now I hope you have a nice day, because the woman who's throat you cut probably won't."

I threw the phone into the wall but it didn't break. I was just putting my thoughts together when I saw a red

Acura pull up in front of my house. Nicky smiled at the driver and trotted down the steps toward him.

Was that the car Rhianna was talking about on the phone? I pulled open my door, bolted down the steps and yelled, "NICKY WAIT!"

CHAPTER 2

MILLI

"What is you doing, nigga? You put the baking soda in first then the Coke! That shit you making don't even look right." Milli told his uncle Kettle.

At forty-six years old, Kettle gave the finest young man a run for his money in the looks department. He kept his body muscular and lean and his dress game couldn't be fucked with.

"I got this shit, Milli. Relax!" he said looking over at him with a slight frown. His muscles pouring out of the white t-shirt he wore. *"Plus you loud ...if somebody was in your hallway they could hear your bitch ass. Don't get mad at me because that shawty making shit hot 'round Kentland for you."*

"Fuck her."

He laughed and said, *"You wilding, neph."*

They both laughed and Milli grabbed a beer from his refrigerator and said, *"Unc, I don't know what to do with them peoples. Niggas 'round the way want Ginger gone."*

"So move her."

31

"She ain't trying to go. She so busy worried 'bout what the fuck I'm doing."

"Then cut her off."

"I might have to."

"She remember yet?"

"Naw. But with the cops being there everyday, niggas can't pump the way they use to. And it's just a matter of time before she remembers and that's going to be more drama. The doctors said her memory lapse is temporary."

When Milli's phone rang, he stepped to the side and answered. "We did what you asked us to do," the girl who threw the bottle in Ginger's window said to him. "And Trixy stepped to her but Ginger whipped her ass. And the cops been around again today."

Milli shook his head.

"You want us to do anything else?"

"Naw...let me stew on some shit for a minute. I'ma get my man to drop that money off for ya'll too for handling that for me."

When he hung up with her he walked back over to Kettle. "Something's gonna have to give 'round Kentland. I might have to do something to Ginger I ain't want to."

Milli's drug business took care of everybody in the family. If he couldn't pump, everybody suffered.

They were still talking when Tracey Knox came home with his daughter Denise. Tracey's beautiful butter colored skin, brown hair and green eyes lit up the room as she waltzed in. She stayed dipped in the finest *fashions including the fifteen hundred dollar Gucci sweat suit she was sporting at the moment, and the four hundred dollar Kate Spade Diaper Bag which swung from her arm.*

The moment Denise saw her father, her face lit up and she made her way to the kitchen.

"Aye, keep her outta here, we cooking," he yelled at Tracey, his eyebrows pulling closely together. "The peoples from CPS already said she got that shit in her system."

Tracey dropped the diaper bag on the floor by the kitchen entrance, and caught Denise before she reached the stove.

Dressed in a cute red shirt with diamond-studded hearts and her jean skirt, Denise was just as pretty as her mother Ginger. Milli scooped Denise up into his strong arms and landed a few kisses on her face.

"Why you being bad as shit? Tracey told me you slapped her today when ya'll were out."

"She told me she was my new mommy," she pointed at Tracey. "And I got a mommy already."

"Oh really," he said giving Tracey an evil glare. Focusing back on Denise he said, "Daddy got you a new doll. Go play with it. It's in your room."

When she was gone he stepped up to his wife and said, "What the fuck you doing? Why would you tell her some shit like that?"

"'Cause...I was thinking, maybe we can raise her together. That way you don't gotta take no more of Ginger's shit." Milli sat on the sofa and Tracey continued,

"Baby, I know you don't wanna talk about this but do you think the courts gonna let us keep Denise? Since Ginger acting up again and stabbed that girl?"

"Why you always gotta ruin shit?"

"I'm not trying to, I just don't want you to be stressed no more."

"Fuck that...it ain't right you trying to fuck my daughter's head up with your bullshit."

"But I'm your wife, and you don't owe Ginger shit! What's keeping you connected to her anyway?" she cried. "I dealt with the fact that you slept with her and got her pregnant days after we broke up, knowing we would be back together," she said getting on her knees in front of him as he remained seated on the couch. "But I'm tired of her calling you over there every five minutes claiming it's about the baby when it ain't. I see the stress on your face. So if Denise stays with us, you won't have to worry."

*"You mean **you** won't have to worry," he said pushing her out of his way, knocking her to the floor. "Maybe if your pussy wasn't so rotten you could have a kid of your own... 'cause we both know that's what this shit's really about."*

"I'm sorry...I just..."

"You just what? The only thing you doing 'round here is overstepping your boundaries. Be glad I'm with you and drop this crusade shit.

Tracey backed away and sat on the sofa. She had no idea that Milli, whom she'd been married to for six years had been with Ginger the same amount of time.

He was dating two bitches simultaneously, and neither one of them was the wiser.

"Now get the fuck outta my face, I gotta holla at Unc."

When she walked sadly into their bedroom, Milli walked into the kitchen with a smirk on his face. He loved dominating.

Kettle looked at him and said, "You playing shit real tight, nephew." He whispered. "You betta be careful."

"I been playing shit tight forever. Tracey ain't gonna do shit but what I tell her." Milli said arrogantly. "And if she was gonna leave she'd be gone by now."

"You don't think that shit gonna catch up with you sooner or later?"

"Naw."

Kettle laughed and Milli said, "What's funny?"

"Nephew, if you wanna be like your father, then be like your father. Don't beat around the bush."

"Fuck you talking 'bout now?"

"You don't think I see how you been carrying shit since he was murdered? The only difference 'tween you and him is that he told his bitches 'bout each other straight up. You went too far with that last situation with Ginger, and it don't look like it's gonna end too good. That's why you in the shit you in now."

"That's where you wrong, my father made a mistake. Had he kept shit on a need to know basis, he'd still be alive today."

Kettle looked at Milli and felt sorry for him. He knew he adopted that same bullshit his baby brother did when he was playing females. His brother called it his C.R.A.W.L Theory and that was, 'If a bitch was not willing to give away her Credit, Respect, Ass, Wealth and Life...she wasn't worth it.'

Milli's father Julius lost his life by adopting that theory when on a hot summer day in June, his main bitch Courtney got tired of the other women, and shot him in the face, along with herself and their two year old twin boys.

"Neph, you got Ginger thinking Tracey's your cousin when she's your wife, and your wife thinking Ginger's your baby's mother instead of your girlfriend. You treading on dangerous ground. Trust me, I know."

"This why a nigga like you don't get me." He paused. "You been married to Pearl's old ass forever. You think they don't know I got somebody else on the side?" He smirked. "Fuck yeah they do. They just don't wanna know the details and it ain't my business to give it to 'em."

Kettle laughed and said, "You got it, nephew."

"I know I got it."

Kettle hesitated and then said, "Question...how you think shit gonna go down with Ginger?"

"I don't know and I don't give a fuck," he said cockily. "'Cause when this shit is all said and done, I won't care if I ever see them peoples again. Don't get me wrong, the pussy was fire, but at the end of the day, she more problems than she's worth."

What Milli didn't know was that while he spoke with his uncle in the kitchen, the bag lying on the floor in the doorway had a baby monitor that Tracey used to keep an ear on Denise inside of it. It was turned on, and the other monitor was in her hand.

CHAPTER 3

GERRON

Most of my shit was already packed so moving wasn't gonna be a problem. And I was so ready to get the fuck outta Kentland it wasn't a joke.

"I can't believe you doing this, man! Kentland all you know, nigga," Bodie said looking up at me from the worn out beige sofa in my living room. At one point people thought we were brothers. We even had the same build, but lately he was getting thinner and it wasn't quite the same. "We ain't even hit the nigga Milli yet!"

"I already told you I'm not fucking with it. Plus shit too hot 'round here right now with the cops coming by all the time."

"You sure it ain't got something to do with you wanting to fuck Ginger?"

"Fuck is you talking 'bout?" I paused. "I might bullshit with her here and there, but that's it." As I was sealing the boxes in my living room, the handle of my gun pressed against my stomach and I placed it on the glass table.

Bodie looked at it and said, "If you 'bout to leave, moe, we might as well hit the nigga first. You passing up on sure bread."

"Nigga, you ain't even hearing me. I'm not fucking with it."

Truthfully I didn't give a fuck if we hit Milli or not, but Bodie was a hot head, and didn't believe in just robbing niggas and going on his merry fucking way. His trigger was loose, he ain't care and I ain't want Ginger to get hurt in the process.

"I'm moving on his ass by myself. Fuck that," he said trying to test my patience.

"You do what you gotta do, playa, you hot anyway and I'm outta here."

Bodie separated seeds from the weed on the table with a matchbook. "I ain't hot, nigga! I'm just smart enough not to pass up on a big payday."

"Smart?" I smirked. "You almost got us nicked twice telling folks who we hitting up. Had it not been for main man getting slumped before he found us, shit coulda got crazy with that last situation."

Bodie rolled the rest of the jay and lit fire to it, when it was hard enough, he allowed the lighter to run over the tip until it turned orange. When I wasn't looking he smirked, and I caught him out the corner of my eye. I was use to that shit though, ever since he started lacing his weed with crack, I ain't trust him. We had been robbing niggas together for 'bout two years. Before him, I kept my work outside of Maryland. But when I got with Bodie, money started rolling in 'cause he always knew when and where major drops was being made. Eventually I found out that he had an inside track. Turns out we was robbing his twin brother Marvel's people, and he'd been looking for us both since.

"Where you moving?" Bodie asked me. "You can at least tell me that."

"Not sure, man. You just take it easy when I do bounce, you might not see thirty if you don't."

"You know somebody could think you was making a threat if they didn't know you," he said pulling on the weed. "Keep telling a nigga he might not see thirty and shit. You might not live to move tonight."

I looked at him and said, "You tripping hard now. Maybe you should put that shit down, before you get yourself hurt."

"Nigga, I'm just fucking with you! You getting all serious and shit. Relax!"

I'm leaving for Vegas on the first flight in the AM 'cause for what I do for a living, I need to be 'round niggas with lots of cash on 'em at all times. And I can't think of a betta place than Nevada.

"So what 'bout your moms?" Bodie continued. "You know she gonna be fucked up 'bout you moving."

I stared out in front of me for a second 'cause he was right. As grimy as this nigga was, when it came to my moms, he was different. He opened doors for her, said 'yes ma'am' this and 'yes ma'am' that. I think he took to her 'cause his mother had been mentally retarded all of her life. She could barely tie her own shoes without help. She got pregnant while in the custody of a mental hospital. She was raped. Her attorney's won her ten million dollars in a lawsuit, and when her twin sons Bodie and Marvel turned eighteen, they spent every last dime of their share. Bodie on getting high and Marvel on keys (kilo) from this nigga in Brooklyn. When they couldn't get any more of her money, they both abandoned her.

"My mother know what it is and I'ma be here every other week to check on her."

"I swear this moving shit is dumb! But you do what you gotta do."

He was still running his mouth when I heard commotion outside. I rushed to the window to see Ginger yelling in a nigga's face, with Nicky and Stevie trying to pull her away.

"Fuck is with that chick?" Bodie asked shaking his head. "I ain't never seen a bitch that fucking feisty before. She better slow down before she get herself killed."

I could tell shit wasn't gonna end right. No sooner then I thought that, did I see this bamma ass nigga drop her. He stole her right in the face.

"Oh shit," Bodie laughed. "That serves her right. He dropped her bitch ass!"

"This nigga can't be for real," I said to myself. I rather a nigga pop a bitch than to hit her in the face.

I moved toward the door and Bodie said, "I know you not 'bout to get in that shit, young! She ain't your fucking problem. She Milli's."

I paid him no attention as I rushed into the street. I caught dude just before he hit Ginger again. I pushed his bamma ass off her, knocking him to the ground instead. He tried to get back up and I dropped him with a hard left.

"Fuck wrong with you, cuz?" he yelled jumping back up. He rubbed his jaw. I drew blood.

Outta nowhere the broad Stevie caught wheels and took off running, leaving her cousin Nicky and Ginger behind.

"Fuck wrong with me? How you look hitting a bitch in the face? What kinda bamma ass shit is that, nigga?"

He laughed and said, "Look at this ole chivalrous ass muthafucka!" Then he paused and said, "You must be sick for putting your hands on me."

I was thinking of dropping him again until he drew his piece. I reached for my gun too but remembered it was on the table in my house. Fuck!

"You got it, young. Ain't no beef here," I said raising my hands.

Ginger got up off the ground and stood behind me. Her mouth was bleeding and I could tell she was trying not to look scared. I hated seeing females hurt.

"You got it, moe. Ain't no need in carrying shit like that. Just go 'bout your business and we gonna go 'bout ours," I told him seriously.

"Oh you making the rules now?" His eyes were rolling around in his head and I could tell he was trying to amp himself up.

"I ain't saying that," I said calmly. "I'm saying you got it, moe."

"Fuck that shit! What you holding, nigga? You know what time it is."

"Hold up, you 'bout to rob me?" I asked frowning.

"Fuck you think? Since you wanna play hero, empty your pockets, QUICK!"

"Young, I ain't 'bout to give you no money."

I looked at his arm and saw a tattoo with the name Treasure on it. His name rings bells. We both stick up niggas so I know this can get ugly if I don't give him what he asking for.

"You gonna empty your pockets on your own," he said cocking his gun, "or do you want me to do it after you drop?" The streets were empty but I knew they were watching.

"Fuck..."

"NIGGA, I'M NOT FUCKING PLAYING 'ROUND WITH YOU! PUT THAT SHIT ON THE HOOD 'FOR I UNLOAD OUT HERE," he screamed. "Don't make the next thing you hear be the clap of my gun. All y'all," he said addressing the girls. "On the hood!"

Instead of putting the shit on the hood, I dropped my money on the ground. "So you being funny huh?" He asked.

"Naw, whether it's on the ground or on the hood, it's still yours right?"

He laughed and said, "Kick that shit over here."

I did, but it only moved a foot.

"You should've stayed your ass inside, man," Treasure continued. "Now you a few bills short." he smirked again like he just came up off of that little bit of money. This nigga's a clown.

"It's all 'bout you, homie," I told him slyly.

"Yeah I know," he laughed at his own joke. "Why ya'll bitches ain't give it up yet? Put the shit on the hood, and don't try to be slick either."

"We 'spose to be friends," Nicky said.

"Don't make me tell you again," he said to her. "I got enough friends."

Nicky put her money on the ground and I saw her face redden. She looked like she was about to cry.

But Ginger must've grew balls 'cause she said, "I can't believe you really 'bout to rob us. This is some stupid ass shit."

"Bitch, give me that bracelet too," he said pointing the barrel at her arm.

"No...I can't...I can't..." He fired a bullet next to where we stood.

"Aye, Ginger, put the shit on the hood," I told her before she got us both killed. If this nigga's hand shook anymore, we were gonna have extra holes in our faces.

She looked at me and reluctantly dropped the money and her bracelet on the hood. I saw the stack she was carrying and knew he came up after all. He stuffed the money in his pockets, and was just about to take my shit until I heard, "BOP, BOP, BOP!"

Bullets flew over our heads and we ducked for cover.

"What the fuck," I said to myself.

When I looked to see where the bullets were coming from, I saw Bodie firing at Treasure who ducked behind his car and fired back. The girls hit the ground too and move behind me to get out of dodge. Bullets flew everywhere. I wanna run but I needed Bodie to move a little closer to Treasure, to give me cover and then I see Bodie has my gun.

"Ya'll 'aight?" I asked looking at the shoot out. "Cause we gotta make a run for it."

"I'm scared," Nicky said.

"Well we ain't got time for that shit, when I tell you to move, run toward the back of Ginger's house."

"Okay," they said.

Treasure continued to unload, but the nigga Bodie was relentless and moved closer toward him. The moment Treasure's attention was taken away from us, I grabbed my money off the ground and yelled, "Move now!"

Me and Ginger dip behind the back of her house and Nicky runs the other way.

"Nicky," Ginger calls out.

"Fuck that bitch," I tell her. "Move!"

Bullets continued to whiz through the air but we finally made it in her backyard. We dipped inside, locked the door and then rushed toward the other side of the house in case bullets came flying into the window.

"Stay down," I told her.

She did and a few minutes later, I heard sirens and the shooting stopped, followed by the sound of slamming car doors. When I heard Bodie's engine rev up, I knew he was gone with my piece. I was gonna definitely have to get up with him before I left town tonight.

I checked the window and said, "They gone. You aight?"

"Yeah. But that nigga got my bracelet! He took my fucking shit," She cried.

"So you not happy you got your life?"

She stood up wiped the tears off of her face and said, "What the fuck just happened?"

"I'll tell you. You started some shit again that's what happened."

She looked surprised and said, "So this my fault?"

"What you expect, shawty? You don't get in a nigga's face unless you ready. You lucky he ain't bust yo ass."

"Hold up, who you talking to?" She said walking up to me.

"Yo ass! You got me in some shit I ain't wanna be in. I was minding my fucking business when you—"

"When you got in *my* business," she said putting her hand on her chest. "I don't recall asking your fucking ass to come save me. And for your information I would've handled that shit with no problem 'cause I ain't got no problem busting my gun too," she said taking it out of her purse which sat on the sofa. It was the new gun she told me Milli bought for her. She put it in her waist and for some reason, the shit turned me on.

"I hate bitches who act like niggas. You can't want a nigga to protect you if you keep faking like you got shit. Which one is it gonna be?"

"Like I said, I could've handled it."

"Anyway, your purse was in here so that shit was useless!"

"Well where was your shit, Mr. Braveheart? I don't see you packing neither. If I'm not mistaking you was ducking on the ground just like me."

If another nigga would've heard the way her mouth popped off he would've walked out.

"You just betta be glad you still breathing."

She waved her hand and said, "Was that Bodie shooting at him?"

"I don't know what you talking 'bout," I said noticing the burn on her floor from earlier. This chick stay with some bullshit.

"Gerron, I know you saw Bodie shooting at dude. He came outta your house."

"Look, some shit need to be left alone," I warned her. "For your own good." If Bodie found out she was saying his name, she could have problems on both of her hands.

When her phone rang, she ran into the kitchen and answered. I could tell by the look on her face that something else was up. This chick stayed with drama. I had to get away from her fast.

CHAPTER 4

GINGER

"I need to know who the fuck you are and I need to know now," I screamed to the girl on my phone.

"I can't tell you. I just wanted to say I'm sorry about what happened."

Click.

When she hung up I rushed outside, ran halfway up my block and banged on Shonda's door with a closed fist. I had to know who that little bitch was calling my house. But the door opened by itself and I walked my uninvited ass inside.

"Shonda!" I said softly. Club pictures of her and Trixy were everywhere. "Shonda, we gotta talk." I whispered.

She didn't answer but I could sense somebody was inside. When I turned the corner leading toward her bedroom, I heard panting and started to go back, but curiosity got the best of me. I never saw her with a man. Once at her bedroom, I couldn't believe what I saw through a cracked door. Trixy was laying on the bed with her legs wide open while Shonda ate her pussy like a side of ribs.

I laughed to myself thinking how she had the nerve to come at me about Milli when she a carpet muncher. I wanted so bad to make myself known but I knew that little tidbit of information would come in handy later.

Although I felt slightly better about my new found secret, I was still dissatisfied about not knowing who this little girl was who decided to make my life miserable. When I walked back into my house, Gerron was still there and he had helped himself to a glass of my Bacardi.

"You want some?" He asked holding the cup out. I took it from him and swallowed it all.

"Everything cool, shawty?"

"Not really," I said looking into his sexy sleepy eyes. I turned away quickly.

"Was that your peoples on the phone? Nicky? Did she get away okay?"

"Oh...no. That wasn't her," I said remembering the shoot out. Too much shit was happening for me to keep up. "Let me call to see if she okay."

My call went straight to voicemail and I was worried.

"She ain't answer," I told him hoping he'd have a response.

"Damn," he said wiping his hand over his face. The sun from my window bounced off of his caramel colored skin and for whatever reason I was horny and knew he had to go. I could feel the seat of my panties getting slick. "Your peoples fine. You just gotta give her a minute to hit you up that's all. We both saw her run away."

Although I was glad Gerron was there for me, it would've been nice to have Milli by my side since he was my man, but he was nowhere to be found and hadn't called back since our argument.

I decided to call him and give him more bad news until Gerron said, "Well let me bounce. I got some shit to do tonight. I'll be over there for a minute if you need me. And then I'm moving...I mean...leaving town."

"You moving?" I said more anxiously than I wanted-ed. "You never told me that."

He smiled and said, "Yeah...why...you upset or something?"

"No...uh...naw...you do what you gotta do. I just didn't know that's all."

"How would you? You don't talk to me."

"You mean you don't talk to me."

Silence.

My mind went to something else that always both-ered me. "Gerron, I know you don't wanna talk about this shit but I gotta know. Are you sure you telling me everything you know 'bout the night I fell and lost my memory? Did you hear anything else from anybody?"

"I ain't answering that shit no more. I already told you I didn't hear shit else."

"Did Milli do something?"

"You don't trust your man?" he asked me.

"I do…I just-"

"Well if you do, just drop it!" He said walking toward my back door.

I rolled my eyes and followed him out. I didn't want him to leave. But he was on his way out until he saw the food on the stove. "Damn, that's all you?"

"If you asking did I cook the answer is yes," I told him.

"Well it looks good, but it probably taste like shit," he joked. "You don't look like you do too well in front of a stove."

"I think you don't know shit about me. I got a baby and a man to cook for, and both of them like to eat which means I can burn."

"That don't mean shit but you know how to turn a stove on."

"You wanna taste it?"

"I can."

"What do I get if it's as good as I know it will be?"

"Whatever you want," he said looking into my eyes.

I cleared my throat and said, "You know what I wanna know."

"Bye, Ginger," he said moving for the door. "I told you I'm not talking about that shit no more."

"Sit down, boy. I'm just fucking with you." I smiled. "Let me show you why I'm wifey material. Now when I'm done with you, I don't want you trying to leave your girl 'cause I'm taken already."

"You ain't telling me shit I don't already know." Plus I ain't got no bitch anyway—"

I cut him an evil look 'cause I was sick of him calling females bitches. Outside of the bedroom anyway.

"I mean, I ain't got no girl. You already know that shit."

"You may not have a girl but I be seeing all them cluckers at your house. Don't forget we cool so there ain't no reason to lie to me."

"I'm single and I like it like that, Ginger."

When he said that I felt some kinda way.

He sat down at my table and said, "You gonna eat with me right?"

Since I hadn't had anything all day, I made a plate and joined him. I wasn't worrying about Milli coming over early, 'cause he never came before eight o'clock at night and it was only three.

"I can tell you was mad at me, but I appreciate you helping me earlier, I know a lot of people would not have done that shit." I said drinking my juice and picking with my food.

"Yeah...me included. I don't know what came over me."

"Well why *did* you help me then?" I said with an attitude.

"Cause he hit you, and ain't no dude 'spose to be hitting no female." I smiled. "How's your face?" he asked me.

"It's cool. Just hurts a little," I said wiping the small scar I had almost forgotten about.

And then I heard raindrops rattling against the kitchen window. The window above the stove was partially open and a gust of wind blew in and knocked a banana shaped calendar magnet from the fridge onto the floor. I closed all the windows in my house. Then I realized I left the window down in my car.

"I'll be right back, Gerron," I said grabbing my car keys from the table. "I left my car windows open and gotta close them."

"You want me to close 'em for you?" He moved like he was going to get up.

"No...just give me a sec." I didn't need people seeing him in my car. It was bad enough he was in my house.

He sat down and I snatched the door open and ran out my back door. A purple haze hovered over my small house and thunderstorms lit the sky. The moment I hit the last step, one of the black heels I was wearing got stuck into the dirt and caused me to fall flat on my face on the damp grass.

As I lifted myself off the ground I heard someone say, "Damn, bitch! You stay falling over! What you can't hold that big ass head up of yours?" Trixy laughed.

"She stay getting shit in her face," Shonda added. "You better watch your step, girly."

When I stood up to see who was talking to me, I saw Trixy and Shonda holding a red umbrella, staring at me over my fence.

"You should know 'bout shit in faces, seeing as though you and Shonda stay eating each other's pussies out."

The smile on her face was wiped clean and both of them hustled up the street. I was so ready to let them know that I was on to their little secret that I wasted a chance to ask Shonda about that mysterious little girl who kept calling my house.

I spit out a few strands of grass, dust my clothes off and run to my car. Then I jump inside my Benz and roll up my car windows. I could see the open kitchen window from my car, and I smile when I saw Gerron stuffing his face. Then it dawned on me, if Milli for whatever reason came home early, I would be busted.

I decided to find out where he was so I turned on my car, and the engine purred like a kitten. Then I picked up the phone from the cradle and dialed his number.

When I heard his voice, my heart sank inside of my chest. "Fuck you want, Ginger?"

"Baby, can we talk? I know why you mad at me and I know it's my fault you thinking about getting rid of me," I said, hitting the vanilla scented tree air freshener dangling from my mirror. "I wasn't trying to make you think I didn't trust you. It's just that so much shit has been happening—"

"Fuck this shit, Ginger. It's over."

Click.

No! It can't be over! I call him back a few times and he doesn't answer. Tears sneak up on me and run down my face. I punched my steering wheel over and over until my knuckles were sore. I lost my boyfriend and I don't know what to do. This shit hurts so badly.

I needed to be alone and decide to get rid of Gerron, so that I can take a bath and clear my mind. So I go back to my house, but Nicky approached me in my backyard. Although the rain pounds on both of us I can still see she's angry.

"Nicky, what happened to you?" I asked examining her body. "Are you 'aight?"

She wiped the water from her eyes and said, "You knew didn't you? You knew that shit was gonna happen today. That's why you were acting funny when we were sitting on your porch. Just tell the truth, Ginger."

"Nick, let's go inside and talk about it. It's raining hard as shit out here."

"Did you know or not?"

"No...I mean yes...I mean, not really..."

"Which one is it?" she said smoothing the wet hair from her face. "I thought we was 'sposed to be friends, Ginger."

"This is gonna sound fucked up, but I had an idea he was gonna do something, I just ain't know what or when. This little girl kept calling my house and told me. I don't know who she is though."

She rolled her eyes and said, "Ginger, why you keep lying?"

"I'm not lying, Nicky! I'm telling you all I know. Some girl called my house and was asking for Shonda's daughter Renee. She said she overheard that someone was gonna set you up, and I tried to warn you. This is not all my fault, don't forget he was supposed to be your friend."

"I don't believe you."

"Have you forgotten that I put my life on the line, lost my bracelet and my money for you?"

When she looked into my back window and saw Gerron fixing himself another unauthorized plate of food she said, "So you fuck with him now? A stick up nigga?"

"You know it ain't even like that, so don't even start no shit."

When Bodie walks up on us out of nowhere, we both jump.

"I ain't mean to fuck ya'll up," he said. "Is Gerron here? I got something for him."

Whenever he was in my presence he made me nervous. "Yeah he inside."

"You mind if I holla at him for a second?"

Since I could see them from where I stood I said, "Go 'head, Bodie. But make it quick."

He looked around a few times and dipped inside. The slam of my screen door rang out a few seconds before stopping.

"Wow, you got the whole crew over here now, huh?" she laughed. "First Gerron and now Bodie?"

"Nick, you my friend, but I'm starting to get real tired of your shit."

"I bet you are," she smirked. "So tell me something, Ginger, how you know they ain't involved? I do recall Gerron grabbing his money off the ground. Why dude didn't get his shit?"

"I don't know 'bout, Bodie but Gerron ain't have shit to do with it.

"Please! Even Stevie saw his ass scoop his money up and run. She the one who put me onto this shit."

"Stevie?" I laughed. "You coming at me with Stevie when she left your ass high and dry out there?"

"Whatever, all I wanna know is why the robber ain't grab Gerron's money when it was on the ground? Why he wait 'til we emptied our pockets and take our shit? Come on, Ginger, everybody 'round here know he bank's people. And if you not careful he gonna do the same shit to you."

"Get out my backyard, Nicky."

She looked at me like she was gonna challenge me, and for the first time ever, I thought about pulling my gun on my friend.

"Don't call me and I won't call you," she said looking behind me at Gerron who was standing in the doorway.

She walked out of my backyard and Bodie walked out the backdoor.

"I appreciate it, sexy," Bodie said. I ignored him.

"What he want?" I asked Gerron. Bodie hopped over my fence. "I never did trust his ass."

"He gave me my piece back. And stay away from him, Ginger. 'Cause I don't all the way trust him either."

CHAPTER 5

GERRON

When we walked into the house her phone rang again and she answered it. I wanted her to ignore that shit because it seemed like every time she picked up the phone, she had bad news.

"Hello?" She exhaled flopping on the sofa.

She looked frightened.

Here comes the bullshit.

So I walked into the kitchen and poured us another drink, because I know after the call she would need it.

"Mr. Claremont, I still haven't heard anything about Leona, I really am so sorry." She paused taking the drink from me. She took a few modest sips before swallowing the whole cup. "Trust me, if I hear anything you'll be the first person I call."

When she hung up the phone I sat next to her and she started crying.

"You 'aight?" I asked.

"I don't understand why all the shit is happening to me! Today has to be the worst day of my life outside of

the day when they took my baby away. And then...."
She sobbed harder, "and then Milli dumped me!"

"That nigga ain't gonna leave you, Ginger so don't worry about that. He just talking shit right now."

"How you know?"

I didn't.

"If he a real nigga, he'd be a fool to let you go over some dumb shit, Ginger. Ya'll been together too long."

"I wish I believed you but he's been acting different lately. And now Mr. Claremont asking me 'bout where his daughter is *again*, and me and Nicky beefing over some bullshit that wasn't my fault." She cried harder. "I don't know what to do!"

"Shit gonna be cool, Ginger. You gotta take shit easy though. You taking on too much at once."

Although I hate seeing females cry, I'm not the best nigga to console 'em either. I'm a gun-toting dude from Kentland, and all I think about twenty-four-seven is getting paper. But here I am feeling like there's nothing more I'd rather do than make her problems go away. I'm 'sposed to be on my way outta Maryland by now, so why am I still here?

"I...I need another drink," she said moving toward the kitchen before her body went limp to the floor, and she's crying again.

I put my drink down, lifted her up and her head fell against my chest. Her body is damp and warm from being caught in the rain. Walking her back over to the couch, I tried to place her down but she gripped me tighter.

"It's going to be 'aight, Ginger. You gotta be strong like you been," I said real slowly. I tried to place her down again but she still ain't let me go.

"Hold me," she sobbed. "Just for a little while. Please."

"I got you," I reassured her.

For whatever reason, her vulnerability turned me on. I'm so use to shawty cussing me out, that I didn't stop to think that she might have a sensitive side. I tried my best to prevent my dick from getting hard but the shit wasn't working. If she stayed in my arms two seconds longer, it was gonna be a wrap, and I was going to be inside of her body.

"Ginger, I ain't trying to disrespect you for real. But if I don't put you down, I ain't gonna be able to help myself. You understand where I'm coming from?"

She looked up into my eyes and said, "Please...I don't wanna be alone right now. Don't make me."

It was over. I moved in for a kiss and she kissed me back. Then I ran my tongue over her lips and gently suck the bottom. Damn, her lips tasted so sweet. I think the alcohol had us on ten, and we ain't give a fuck.

"You sure 'bout this?" I asked because I didn't want a drunk fuck. I wanted a full participant.

When she doesn't respond I slip my tongue back into her warm mouth. While our lips connected her tears rubbed against my face. She ain't crying no more though.

I tried to place her down again but this time she let me and pulled me toward her. I threw the sofa pillows on the floor and fell between her warm legs. The handles of our guns clank each other and we took them out, placing them on the floor next to the couch. Then I remembered, I'm in this dude's house. What if he came in here and shit got outta hand? I'd be forced to kill him when I'm dead wrong for dicking his bitch down.

"I'ma have to take a rain check, sweetheart," I said lifting up.

Her eyes look sad and she said, "So you gonna leave me like this?"

"You know I want you, but if your folks come in here, I'ma have to bust his ass. I don't wanna dead dude when I know how you feel 'bout him."

"I told you we not together no more," she said lifting her shirt freeing her titties. "And I want you to make love to me."

"So just like that, it's over?" I ain't never ask a bitch these many questions when offered the pussy, but there was something 'bout Ginger I wanted and I didn't want to start something we wouldn't finish.

"Right now I don't even give a fuck about Milli. So what *we* gonna do?"

I smiled and softly sucked her nipples, one and then the other. That was my way of answering her question. She grabbed my head and pulled me closer to her body, I could smell her sweet perfume.

We were all over each other and then she disconnected.

61

"Stop," she said under her breath.

This chick just gave me some bullshit 'bout not giving a fuck and now she want me to stop? I acted like I ain't even hear that shit.

"Stop, Gerron...please," she said louder.

I sat up and put my gun in my waistband.

She adjusted her shirt and folded her hands over her breasts. "I shouldn't even be doing this shit with you."

I frowned at her. "Then why are you?"

"'Cause I'm sick of Milli playing games with me! He act like he don't even care."

I stood up and said, "Well as much as I'd love to console you, I ain't Oprah. I'm 'bout to bounce. I'll get up with you when I can."

"So what...you mad now?" she yelled.

"Shawty, five seconds earlier we was 'bout to fuck and now we not. You say the nigga Milli dumped your ass and you got me sucking all over your titties and shit like I'm an infant. Then you tell me to stop. You tell me if you think I'm mad or not."

"Ugggh," she said frowning. "So what...if a bitch don't fuck you, you carry shit like that? Like you got an attitude or something?"

"Naw...but if a bitch was 'bout to fuck me and stopped, yeah, that's how I carry it."

I moved toward the door and she said, "I knew you was a cruddy ass nigga the moment I saw your eyes."

"Call it what you want, but the one thing I don't play is games." I tried to convince my dick to go down and said, "I hope everything works out." Truthfully I didn't give a fuck.

My hand was on the doorknob when she said, "I still want you to stay, G."

I turned around to look at her and said, "Come on, Ginger. You fucking me up with this bullshit. I'm not 'bout to sit up in your face and pretend we twins when I just finished sucking your titties. If all this shit ain't happen it would be cool 'cause that's how we got down anyway, but all this shit *did* happen. All I want to do right now is take a cold shower, and head up the road."

I opened the back door and stepped into her backyard. I was five seconds from hopping over my fence when she said, "If you stay, it'll be worth your while. I promise."

CHAPTER 6

GINGER

I don't know why, but for some reason I felt like we connected on a deeper level. Even though he can be mean, cocky and straightforward, but at least you know where he's coming from.

He walked back toward the couch and sat down. I sit next to him and could smell Dolce & Gabbana cologne.

"I wasn't trying to play games, I just feel like a whore," I whispered to him. "I didn't mean to make you angry."

"What's wrong with being a whore?" He joked.

"I'm serious, Gerron," I said hitting his arm.

"Like I said, what we do between us will be between us. Me, myself...I love a nasty bitch." He cleared his throat. "I mean, a chick who knows what she wants in the bedroom."

I heard what he was saying but something didn't sit right with me.

"Umm...uh...did you or Bodie have something to do with what happened today, with the robbery? I know

I asked you before but I gotta know for real. I know you...you know, do that kind of shit all the time."

He frowned and said, "You know what...yeah it's true, I rob dealers for their paper, but I would never turn my gun on somebody I fuck with. Plus how was I involved when the nigga tried to rob me too? Come on, Ginger...you way smarter than that."

"You right," I smiled placing his gun back on the floor. "I am."

He pulled me toward him and said, "Now get your sexy ass over here and stop worrying 'bout the bullshit. The longer you make me wait, the badder it's gonna be when I get up in that thang."

I glanced at the door and said, "I can't wait."

He looked at the door also and said, "That nigga ain't coming in here is he?"

"Naw, he said it's over, so let it be over."

He got serious with me and said, "Ginger, I'm 'bout to move, so after we do what we do, you ain't gotta worry 'bout seeing me no more and the nigga Milli won't ever know what happened if ya'll get back together. Your secret and your body is safe with me. So let's take care of each other right now, and worry 'bout all that other shit later. Cool?"

No longer waiting for my confirmation, he removed my shoes and started massaging my feet. His hands felt warm and his strokes were long, and passionate. I've had massages before but this took the cake. Who knew a nigga who was probably a murderer could be so passionate? Unable to resist, I dropped my head back and let him do his thing.

"Hmmmm," I exhaled. "That feels so nice."

During the entire time Milli and I had been together, he never touched any part of my body outside of my breasts, ass and pussy. So I was caught off by Gerron's touch and was tempted to drift off into an erotic sleep. Until...he placed three of my toes into his warm mouth, his wet tongue circled each of them. At first it tickled, and I wasn't sure if I'd be able to take it but then he applied a little pressure with his strokes. Ummm it was just right.

"Damn that shit feels so fucking good." My pussy jumped. "You must do this a lot."

"What I tell you 'bout worrying about bullshit?" He winked and continued his work. "Tonight is about me and you."

My juices coated my panties and suddenly I became jealous of the attention my toes were getting. I wondered if he could do the same thing to my pussy and if it would feel as good.

"You got some sexy ass feet," he said staring into my eyes. "I wonder how you taste."

He looked at me with hunger in his eyes and tugged at the bottom of the jeans I was wearing. I assisted by raising my body up off the couch just a little, dropping back down when he had my panties and jeans off. Then he pushed my legs apart and stared into my wetness. I shivered from nervousness, and excitement. I couldn't believe I was really about to fuck Gerron...my homie...my friend.

"Damn...it's prettier than I thought."

"Am I too wet for you?"

"How you sound?" He took one finger and pushed it deeper into my cave. My legs tensed and he said, "Relax, Ginger. This is going to be good."

I obeyed and he covered my clit with his warm mouth. As his finger went in and out of me, his tongue circled my clit and I felt my body shake. If he kept it up I was gonna cum.

"Ummm...*and* your pussy sweet." He looked at my pussy like he never saw one before, but I guess he'd never seen mine. All the talks we had on the porch at night, and this is what it finally came to. Him and I together. I guess we both knew it would happen sooner or later.

"I've fucked some chicks in my day, but I ain't never seen a bitch with a body as bad as yours."

Pushing my legs further apart, he moved in and sucked my clit again flickering his tongue wildly. My body sunk into the couch and he pulled me closer to his mouth.

"Ahhh....Gerron...I...I wanna...cum so badly."

I placed my hand on the back of his head. His tongue moved from the tip of my clit to my asshole. Back and forth, back and forth he was nice and slow. I released my titties from my shirt and sucked them one at a time, something I did when I played with my pussy in the house alone.

"Damn you look sexy doing that shit," he complimented me eying my work instead of his own.

"Lick this pussy, baby. Don't stop, mothafucka. You betta work that shit."

With that he slid two fingers into my slippery wetness and I maneuvered my waist around them. I no longer cared who he was and for the first time ever, I would break the rules…all of them. If Milli wanted to act like a bitch, FUCK HIM! I was gonna do me too.

As if two fingers weren't enough, he placed three inside me, then four and then five. Surprisingly enough my sex-deprived pussy took them all.

I was on the verge of letting the rest of my wetness flow over his fingers until he placed his mouth back on my clit and licked up more of the icing that oozed from my wet cave. His tongue felt like warm water and on everything I love, before he even fucked me, I was having the best sex of my life.

CHAPTER 7

GERRON

The scent of her pussy was intoxicating...something like an aphrodisiac but better. Still on my knees, I removed my mouth and felt her legs tremble.

"You okay?" I asked placing my hand on her brown thighs.

"Y...yes, you got me feeling so good." I had played the tongue flicking game long enough and it was time to fuck.

I released myself from my pants and she sat up and said, "I have to *taste inspect* this thing first."

She got on her knees and licked the tip slowly, looking up at me with those cat eyes. Staring down at her pretty face ain't do nothing but get me harder. She licked the shaft up and down, side-to-side and left to right. Then she grabbed the side of my legs and pushed her mouth all the way down my dick. Damn! No gagging.

"Damn, bitch! You killing that shit, huh?"

She looked up at me, and continued her deep throat skills.

"I need to feel that pussy." I said.

She smiled, turned around and got on all fours. Oh shit! You can't be serious! Shawty's fuck game can't be this official. Stroking my wet dick one more time, I pushed halfway inside her pussy and felt her walls closing in on my joint.

"Damn, bitch! I shoulda been hitting this shit a long time ago."

I pulled my dick out real quick, spread her wet pussy lips apart and slammed into that pussy full force. She tensed up and I pulled her back to me. I wanted to feel all of her with no hold back.

"Don't fucking move again! You gonna take this shit right here."

"Okay...okay," she moaned. "I ain't trying to go nowhere, baby. Just keep doing that shit right there."

"You just keep that ass up in the air like that, and I'll do the rest."

I eased out of her halfway and pushed back into that thang again. I was hard as a block of ice and I saw her body tense up. "You know I'm gonna bang your back out for making me wait so long right?"

She licked her fingers and smiled. "Tonight, this pussy is all yours and you can treat it how you want."

Lifting her ass cheeks up, I pushed fully into her and together we worked as smooth as the engine on a Bentley. She wasn't sposed to feel this fucking good. The nigga Milli must be crazy.

"Dammmn, girl" I pulled her closer and she bit down on the bottom of her lip. "You trying to make a nigga remember this shit ain't you?"

She grinned and bucked her hips wildly. Damn she sexy and thick in all the right places.

"Turn over on your back," I demanded.

When she did, I took her legs and put them straight up in front of me in the air. Then I closed 'em, grabbed her ankles and banged in and out of that thang. When I felt myself cumming, I let her legs drop over my right shoulder and decided to murder that pussy.

Smack. Smack. Smack. Smack.

"Damn, Gerron," she moaned. You fucking the shit outta this wet box ain't you?"

That pussy was making all kinds of sounds.

Slurp. Slurp. Slurp. Slurp.

"What you think…I was playing?"

She bucked wilder, her titties were moving all over the place. She held one in her hand and sucked the nipple again. I love that shit. She was trying to go down as the best bitch I ever fucked in my life, and things were looking good for her.

"Gerron, that's it, baby! Pound that shit! I like it rough! I'ma make you wanna fuck me again before you leave town."

"Bet that," I responded biting my bottom lip.

My body shivered and she said, "Please don't cum yet, I want this shit to last."

I heard her but there was nothing else I could do. She was getting wetter and wetter and I was almost

there. We gripped each other and her movements became swifter and wider while mine went harder and
longer. She was raining on my dick and I spread her
thighs apart, dropped my head back and it was over.

"Awwwww….shitttttt!"

"Just five more seconds," she begged. "Please."

I tried to think of everything in the world except
the bad bitch up under me. But the more she begged and
moved, the closer I was to busting a nut. And then she
said, "I'm cuuuuummmmmmmin'! Oh my Gawd I'm
cuuuuummmmin'."

I was cumming too and pushed into her hard one
last time, nutting all in her wet pussy. I fell on her warm
body and she was breathing heavily in my ear.

"You okay?" I asked. "I ain't knock nothing out
the way did I?"

She laughed and said, "You were GREAT but I
think my pussy will survive." Then she wrapped her
arms around me holding me closer and I felt she didn't
want me to leave. We kissed. "We fuck good together,"
she told me.

"You got that shit right," I responded.

My phone rang on the floor and I saw it was
Bodie. He was getting on my nerves and it was starting
to make me uneasy.

"Look, I'm 'bout to go." I said pulling my pants
up.

"So you gonna leave me like this?" she frowned.

Right before I answered I heard keys jiggle at her front door. We both whipped our heads in the direction of the sound and jumped up to our feet.

Ginger said, "Oh shit! Milli's here..."

CHAPTER 8

GERRON

Today was wild as shit and I couldn't believe I let Ginger almost get me late. I was supposed to be on the road a long time ago and if I didn't hurry up, I was gonna miss my fucking flight. Fuck was I thinking breaking that chick's back out at her crib? Where her dude be most of the time?

When I opened my back door to my house, I gripped my weapon 'cause something ain't feel right. Good thing Bodie brought my piece by Ginger's earlier. I had robbed so many niggas it could be anybody. Aimed, I walked deeper toward the living room and flipped on the light switch. I was slow and careful. When the lights came on, I saw someone sitting on my sofa and I cocked my gun.

"Relax, nigga. It's just me," Bodie said squinting his eyes. "I was just taking a nap until you got here. What time is it anyway?"

"Nigga is you tripping?" I was so mad my muscles bulged in my neck. "Fuck you doing at my crib?"

"I been here since I left that bitch's house earlier," he said lighting a cigarette. "You can't tell me you ain't fuck that bitch now. You peed for that pussy didn't you, playa?" He laughed. "You was over there for too long, man."

"Bodie, what I do with my dick is my business." I tucked my gun into my waist. "You still ain't answer my question. Fuck you doing at my house?"

"Shit was too hot back at my place...you know... after the shoot out and all. I didn't know if the cops were trying to get at me. So I stayed here."

"The shoot out happened 'round here, if anything shit hotter here than at your spot."

"Relax, nigga, I'm 'bout to go anyway. Just wanted to make sure you okay that's all."

This dude was tripping and I ain't never seen him like this before. "Good, 'cause I'm 'bout to head up the road."

Bodie stood up and walked toward me. "So you still not gonna tell me where you going, huh? All the jobs we pulled off and I don't even get to know that?"

I laughed, grabbed my bag from the back and said, "You gotta go, B. I'm already running late."

When I came back out Bodie frowned, placed his hand heavily on my shoulder and said, "I bet you told that bitch where you moving didn't you?"

"Nigga get the fuck off me!" I said pushing him away. He fell against the wall, and dusted his shirt off.

He frowned and I knew if he hadn't pawned his gun, he would've used it on me. But I tapped the handle of my rod on my waist so my message could be clear.

He looked at it and said, "I can still smell her pussy on you."

"Bodie, the door!" I said gripping my weapon. "Don't make me say it again 'cause I won't!"

He looked at the door, back at me and said, "So I guess we not hitting the nigga Milli together huh?

Silence.

"Well I guess I got to do it myself," he continued. "You made a wrong move, G. A wrong move for coming at me like that." He walked out the door and I slammed it behind him.

CHAPTER 9

GINGER

I never saw somebody move as quickly as Gerron. I guess years of sticking niggas for their money paid off 'cause by the time Milli turned the knob, Gerron was out the back door and I was in the bathroom faking like I was using it.

"Ginger! Where the fuck you at?" Milli said rustling in the living room area. "And why the fuck are pillows on the floor? And why is the floor burned?"

My heart dropped. "The floor got burned from the fire I was telling you about. And the pillows on the floor because I was laying on the floor watching TV!"

"Come out here! We gotta talk."

I wiped my pussy in the sink and all I was thinking was, why the fuck is he even here? Didn't he dump me? All I had on my mind was Gerron.

FUCK A MILLI!

When I was clean and in the right frame of mind, I took a deep breath, walked into the living room and put a fake smile on my face. But the moment I saw his expression, and how smooth his stance was, I wondered if

I'd made a big mistake. There was no denying I still had feelings for him. He looked so good.

"Fuck wrong with you?" Milli asked sitting on the sofa, a large blue duffel bag hung from his hand. I knew it was the package for the soldiers he had working for him in Kentland. "Why you over there looking all crazy and shit?"

"Huh?"

"Huh?" he said sarcastically. He dropped the bag on the floor and rested his gun on the table. "I asked you a fucking question. What's wrong with you?"

"Nothing, baby." I walked to my purse to grab a stick of gum. "I'm surprised you here that's all. I mean, I thought it was over between us."

"Whateva...you know ain't nobody leaving you yet. But shit ain't safe for you no more. That's what I wanted to come talk to you about. I'm moving you out of the neighborhood."

"Okay." I said not feeling like fighting. I just had the best fuck of my life and I wanted to savor the moment. "I'll move."

"Where's your bracelet?"

I rubbed my wrists. I forgot all about it. "I got robbed today."

"Was they trying to rob me instead?" he asked with lowered eyebrows.

"No." I said rolling my eyes. He didn't even give a fuck about me. This was all about him.

"I bet that nigga, Gerron was involved. I'ma have somebody smoke his ass."

"NO!" I yelled louder than I wanted to. "He wasn't even home at the time."

"How the fuck you know?"

Oh shit, I fucked up. "I'm not sure, I just don't think Gerron had anything to do with it. He helped save me."

"You know what, just fix my fucking plate while I sort some shit out. While you at it be thinking 'bout five good reasons I should keep ya ass around."

How could I think of any reasons? I wasn't even sure if I wanted to stay around anymore. When I walked into the kitchen he followed me and an evil glare spread across his face.

"Who the fuck been in my house?"

When I turned my head and saw two plates and two cups on the kitchen table I felt like busting myself in the mouth.

"Nicky's greedy ass must've been over," he said answering his question for me.

I felt as if a huge weight had been lifted off my shoulders. "Uh yeah...Nicky was here."

"Well you coulda cleaned up...pillows on the floor, dishes on the table, damn! Don't start getting nasty and shit, Ginger because I don't play that shit."

My patience was running thin with him and then his phone rang. From where I stood I saw his cousin Tracey's name flash on his iPhone and remembered I hadn't had a chance to ask him about Denise, our daughter.

He stepped a few feet away from me and said, "What, Tracey?"

He was silent as he paced the floor. "Well I don't know what I'm gonna do right now." He looked at me out the corner of his eye and then turned around probably so I couldn't read his lips. I followed him into the living room hoping he'd give me some info about my baby.

"Well I 'ont feel like talking right now. You shouldn't have been trying to be slick by listening to my conversation."

"Milli...is that Tracey?" He threw his hand up in the air. "Can I talk to her? I wanna speak to my baby."

"Didn't you see my hand go up?" He asked covering the phone. I nodded. "Then shut the fuck up."

Directing his attention back to Tracey he said, "I'll rap to you later, now is not a good time."

Their conversation sounded weird and something didn't sit right with me.

"I don't know if you realize it or not, but Denise is with my cousin Tracey, that was her on the phone just now," he said sitting back in the kitchen eating his food.

"Is everything okay 'cause I wanted to talk to Denise?"

"Everything cool and Denise's sleep right now. I'll call back tomorrow so you can speak to her. But don't worry, she's good."

I frowned. "But I wanna speak to her now."

"Tracey, relax! I said I'll call her for you tomorrow."

"Tracey?" I repeated leaning in toward him. I was so angry my head begin to throb. "My name is Ginger."

"You know what I meant. I get ya'll names mixed up sometimes."

I don't believe him. Why don't I believe him? Who confuses their girl with their cousin?

"Is everything cool between us, Milli?"

"You gotta ask yourself that since you don't listen to me, Ginger. You quick with the mouth and you got a temper. Its cause of you CPS took my kid."

"They saying she got crack in her system," I responded. "Ya'll cooking 'round her when she be at your house? Because I don't come near that shit so it wasn't me, Milli."

"Fuck no we don't cook around her." He paused. "And what happened to your face? That nigga who robbed you hit you in your face too?"

"Yeah."

He laughed and said, "See...that's the shit I be talking 'bout." He pointed at me and shook his head. "Everybody not gonna let you run off at the mouth without consequences and repercussions. At some point you gonna get paid back."

He didn't even ask if I was okay. What kind of boyfriend is that? I was five seconds from telling him how I felt when I saw a dude walk through my back door with a ski mask on. He locked the door and aimed the gun in our direction.

In a distorted deep voice he said, "I'ma make this quick. Get me the bag over there on the floor. If you do it slow I'm taking your lives instead."

Milli tried to move for his gun but the robber yelled, "Don't fucking move, nigga! This not a game. I'm a certified killer."

I was so scared I fumbled around, and fell against the stove. When Gerron left earlier after we fucked, I didn't have time to lock the back door and now I'd have to pay for it.

"I don't even know what you talking 'bout man," Milli said. "That ain't shit but dirty laundry. I brought it over here so my girl could clean it. You don't want that shit. Trust me."

"Stop fucking 'round! I already know what it is."

"Fuck," Milli said slamming his fist down onto the table. Food plopped off of his plate and slapped on the table and the floor. "Why the fuck you ain't lock the back door, Ginger?" He looked at me. "Why you got me in here with open doors when you know how much money I'm worth?"

Although the robber spoke in his fake voice I knew it was Bodie. I never could stand that grimy ass nigga! I was still cussing him out in my mind when I smelled Dolce & Gabanna cologne. The smell was so strong it reminded me of the lovemaking session I just experienced earlier. And then my heart dropped. It was him.

"Gerron, is...is...that you?" I hesitated hoping it wasn't true.

Silence.

My eyes moved from the Jordan's he was wearing that sat next to my Dior heels earlier on the floor, and the jeans I helped take off to release his dick. Then I glanced at the hand holding the weapon, which had recently been all over my body. He betrayed me and it burned so badly.

"Why you doing this shit, Gerron?" I tried not to cry but I could feel the tears bubbling.

He took the mask off and said, "I'm sorry, 'bout this shit, Ginger, I know you don't believe me but I gotta do this."

The pain I felt in my heart hurt more than I could explain or ever would imagine. "But what about...I mean....everything else?"

"All I can say is sorry," he said not looking at me directly. "If I could tell you why right now I would."

"Nigga, do you know what I could do to you?" Milli asked breaking the moment. "Do you have any idea on how many niggas I know? You must have a wish to die."

Gerron looked at him and said, "Yeah, I know about you and if I gave a fuck I wouldn't be in your house sticking a gun to your face." He paused. "Ginger, hand me the bag and don't try no shit, or I'll blow this nigga's head off." He looked at my gun and Milli's.

"Fuck you, moe," Milli yelled at him. "Ginger, don't give this nigga shit!"

Gerron fired, shooting Milli in the arm. "Ahhhhhh," Milli screamed. "You shot me!"

"The bag," Gerron said looking at him then at me. "Give it to me."

"Ginger, give this nigga the work," Milli said holding his bloodied arm. He focused on Milli. "I sho hope you leaving town, slim. 'Cause I betta never see your face 'round here again."

"Well maybe I should take care of you right now and you won't have to worry about looking for me later. I could put you out of your misery you know?"

"Gerron, please," I said softly. "Don't shoot him again. I'm gonna give you what you came for."

Milli bit his lip and I slowly walked toward the bag. I still felt the sting of Gerron's betrayal on my chest but I had to put it away. As I was walking toward Gerron with the duffle, I saw the pillows on the floor, which were reminders of our love session and I grew angry. Who was he to play me like this? They say I got a temper. Well I'm about to explode. I was about to speak my mind when my house phone rang.

I moved to answer it and Gerron said, "Don't do that, Ginger. Bring the bag, I gotta go."

"Don't say my name out your mouth again," I screamed with the phone in my hand. "Ever!"

"Ginger don't make me..."

"What? Shoot me? Go 'head Gerron 'cause I don't even give a fuck no more!"

Gerron looked at me and said, "Why you gotta make shit so fucking difficult? You knew who I was when we met. Didn't you tell me that I'm a stick up dude about five times today alone? Why you in your feelings?"

"Because I thought you had a code."

When the phone rang again I decided to answer whether he threatened me or not. I placed my head against the receiver and someone said, "Hello."

"Can I speak to Ginger?"

"Is this Rhianna?" I asked hesitantly.

"Yes, but I'm ready to tell you who I really am now."

Despite everything that was going on at that moment, I still wanted to know and I wanted to piss Gerron off too by delaying the situation despite him having a gun on us. "Go 'head. "

"My name is Melissa Rice but everybody calls me Melli. And Stevie is my mother."

"Melissa Rice?" I frowned. "Which one of Stevie's daughter's are you?"

I saw discomfort in Milli's eyes when I said her name, and I wondered was it because of the pain he was feeling or something else.

"Ginger, hang that shit up and give this nigga the bag," Milli interrupted. "I ain't got no time for this shit right now." Blood poured out of his arm. "I'm gonna need to go to the hospital."

"I'm her middle daughter," Melissa said. "The one you think is retarded."

Silence.

This was getting weirder. "Melissa, I'm in the middle of something. So tell me what you gotta say, because I don't have a lot of time."

"I want to tell you…I want to tell you…that my father is Milli."

My heartbeat fast and my eyes found their way to Milli's.

"What do you mean Milli's your father?" I asked loud enough for him to hear my voice.

"He's my daddy. But I don't see him all the time, not as much as I want to anyway."

"Melli are you saying that my boyfriend is your father," I asked for clarification. And sure as the breath went in and out of my body, Milli's skin looked flushed and I knew she was right.

"Who the fuck is that on the phone?" Milli asked. "Somebody lying on me again? I told you to stop believing these bitches around here, Ginger. I wish you start listening to me instead of them."

And then I remembered, earlier in the day when I told Milli about the fight with Trixy. When we were on the phone he said, *"Why you can't walk away from the ordinary and step up when necessary? You acting young and dumb, always believing these bitches when they tell you I fucked them."*

Either he already knew about the fight somehow before I told him about it, or he fucked Trixy like she said. Because I never got the chance to tell him the details of why we were fighting before he made that comment.

I swallowed hard and said, "I gotta go, Melli."

Milli looked uneasy and not angry like he did when he first came home. Tears filled my eyes and ran down my cheeks. All the lies, all the games had finally caught up with him. I spent all of this time being with a man who couldn't give a fuck about me and the entire neighborhood knew but me. He fucked everybody right in my face. No wonder they didn't care about me being with him. He was everybody's man.

"Is Melli telling the truth?" I asked Milli softly. "Are you her father?"

"Have you forgotten we getting robbed in here, Ginger? Do you really want to do this now?"

"We ain't getting robbed nigga, *YOU* getting robbed," I yelled still holding onto the bag. "Now I need to know and I need to know now, are you the father of one of Stevie's kids!"

"No," he said sternly. And for some reason I was temporarily relieved. "I'm the father of *ALL* of her kids."

I stumbled backwards and was just about to fall against my glass table when Gerron stepped behind me and caught me. He had the gun aimed at Milli in one hand and my body in the other.

"You 'aight?" he asked holding me up, but making sure to keep his eye on Milli too.

"Yeah...I'm just...I'm just..."

"Stupid," Milli yelled. "Why the fuck you worried 'bout what I do with somebody else when I take care of you? Look at everything you have 'round here. Look at the whip you driving out front and the purses in your closet. You don't want for shit, Ginger. Any other bitch would kill to be in your shoes."

Gerron released me and my chest tightened. Nothing he was saying was making me feel any better. I gave up everything for him and it was a complete waste of my time. I snapped and the next thing I knew, I was waving wild punches that landed on Milli's face. Gerron whisked me up and held on to me until I calmed down but I smacked him in the face too. I was angry at everybody. I was angry for giving a fuck, and I was angry for not being able to see Milli for the man that he really was.

"Before I die, I'm gonna make sure you wish you'd never put your fucking hands on me, Ginger," Milli promised. "After all the shit I did for you, to keep you outta jail this is how you repay me."

"What the fuck are you talking about to keep me outta jail? You sell crack cocaine not me!"

"I'm out," Gerron said grabbing the bag out of my hand. For a moment I forgot he was even in the room. "I'ma leave ya'll to it."

When Gerron moved toward the door I felt like I could barely breathe I was crying so hard. I swallowed hard and said, "Take me with you, Gerron."

Both Milli and Gerron looked at me like I'd lost my mind.

"What?" Gerron asked. "You don't even know where I'm going." But I saw in his eyes he was considering my request. I just needed him to say yes.

"Please, I can help you, maybe be a look out or something. Nothing's here for me in Kentland any more."

"Ginger, you need to calm down and relax," Milli said. "You acting real dumb right now. He's a stick up nigga. He don't give a fuck about you."

I ignored him, took two steps closer to Gerron and said, "I'm begging you to take me with you. I don't even care where we going. We connected tonight Gerron, and I know you got feelings for me like I have feelings for you too. I want to get away from here. Take me with you."

Silence.

Gerron looked me in the eyes. He wanted to say okay, I felt it in my heart. "Look, I know stuff's messed up for you and your peoples, but my lifestyle ain't for you and your little girl," Gerron said angrily. "I gotta go."

He was right, but it still hurt.

With that Gerron held on tightly to the bag and backed out the door with the gun aimed in our direction. When the door slammed I felt my chances of escaping go with him too.

"You's a stupid bitch!" Milli laughed standing up. He reached for the phone. "Got a nerve to get mad with me 'cause of some bitches I fucked." When he said bitches I could only imagine how many there were. "There's a luxury tax when you fuck with rich niggas like me, Ginger. You gotta recognize that shit. "

In that moment, that he quoted a phrase Nicky always used, my memory came flooding back to me. Everything that I forgot during the last night I saw my best friend. I remembered being as upset as I am now, and standing in this living room.

It was Milli all along.

SIX MONTHS EARLIER

Carolyn pulled her Cadillac in front of her daughter's house in Kentland. They were home one day early from vacation, and both of them were exhausted.

"Baby, you sure you don't want to stay with me another night?" Carolyn asked Ginger as she parked. "I hate you leaving me so soon."

"I'm sure, ma. Plus I wanna surprise Milli. I know he misses me."

Ginger's mother sighed and looked in the back seat at her granddaughter who was sound asleep.

"So what time are you gonna pick her up Friday?"

"I'll be there in the late afternoon." Ginger said grabbing her overnight bag. She reached in and gave her mother a kiss on the cheek. "I had a good vacation with you. And I can't wait to do it again."

Carolyn smiled and said, "Me too, baby and I don't want ya'll fighting tonight. If you feel you're going to get into an argument with him, come back over my house instead."

"I will, ma. But everything is going to be fine."

"Call me later," Carolyn replied.

When she pulled off, Ginger turned around to look at her house. The lights were off but she could see the glow from the TV in the living room. She waved at Gerron who was sitting on his front steps smoking a jay. When he spotted her moving toward her house he rushed toward her. It was as if he was trying to prevent her from going inside.

"Hey...hang out with me for a sec, Ginger," he said anxiously.

"Not now, Gerron. I just got back in town."

"Ginger, please. Just for a minute." He gripped her arm.

"Later, Gerron." She said snatching away from him. *"Stop being so crazy."* She wondered what was his problem as she walked inside of her house.

When Ginger opened the door, she saw the back of the sofa in the middle of the floor. She smiled when she saw Milli's back raise up, and the glow of the TV bounce against his chocolate skin. Her pussy jumped as she anticipated what she was going to do to him. That was until she saw a woman's pink fingernails digging into the flesh of Milli's back.

"Damn, ya'll feel good," he said.

When Ginger looked on the floor there were eight shoes scattered everywhere.

"Milli," Ginger said walking further into the house. Milli hopped up off of the sofa and so did the woman he was fucking.

Ginger was devastated when she saw her best friend Leona naked and standing at his side.

"Oh, my God," Leona said covering her mouth. "Ginger, I'm so sorry. I didn't know you were coming home early. Please forgive me."

While Ginger's heart beat heavy in her chest, the only people she saw was Leona and Milli at the moment.

"Fuck you doing here with my man, bitch?" Ginger screamed. Turning her attention to Milli she said, "And what are you doing with my best friend? How could you two do me like this?"

"It's not what you think," Milli said with his semi-hard dick swinging. "You been gone for a week and we missed you. So we were talking 'bout you and one thing lead to another." He threw the covers over the couch and looked down again. Ginger wondered why.

"And so you fucked my best friend," Ginger questioned. "Is that what you're telling me?"

Ginger pulled the gun out of her purse and aimed at her best friend. "Why, Leona?" The gun shook in her hand. "When you knew how much I went through with this dude! I loved you."

"I'm sooooo sorry," Leona sobbed.

"Sorry isn't good enough." Ginger fired a bullet into Leona's head and she didn't flinch once. Her body dropped on the floor and made a thumping sound.

When her body fell, Nicky and Stevie, who were also on the couch but hiding, popped up off the floor. Ginger refocused on the shoes and saw that they were four different styles. She was so angry that she didn't *notice that before. Overwhelmed, she ran outside, lost her balance and hit her head on the step of her house. She passed out cold.*

After pulling Ginger inside, Milli, Nicky and Stevie who were participating in the sex game for money, buried Leona's body in Virginia in an effort to hide the crime. Milli did not want her found with his DNA inside of her body, and Leona would never be seen again.

When I remembered what happened I was angry and hurt all over again. Milli was never in my corner. He was always for self, and now I could see that. I'm devastated.

"It was you that night! You fucked my best friends…and I caught you. You fucked Leon and Nicky, the only friends I ever cared about! Why?"

He smirked and said, "So you finally remember, huh?"

"You fucking bastard! You dirty dick bastard! Why?"

"Because I'm a man and I wanted to," he yelled. "This is my world, Ginger not yours. Besides you wasn't supposed to come home that night! And as far as burying Leona I did you a favor! You murdered that bitch and it's because of me getting rid of the body that you aren't doing time in the feds right now. You should be on your knees thanking me instead of getting on my fucking nerves." He gripped his arm. "You realize how much time you would've gotten had she been found?"

"I'm going to tell the police it was you," Ginger promised. "They'll believe me."

"Her body will never be found, but if it does I got the gun you used in case you ever act up. That's why I bought you a new one."

Angry I grabbed the new gun he was just talking about and held it in my hand. I committed murder before. I wondered if I could kill again. I tested the theory when I bust him five times in the chest. I guess I was capable after all. Milli fell to the floor and more blood oozed from his body. Thanks to me he was a holey mess.

"What you say, Milli?" I asked standing over him. "I'm a what? You said earlier that someone would KILL to be in my shoes, I guess you were right."

I grabbed his cell phone from his pocket and scrolled through his contact list. I had to get my baby from that bitch Tracey and leave town. I found her number and called.

"Milli?" Tracey said anxiously thinking I was him probably. "We need to talk." I could tell by her voice that she was fucking him. I guess he had no limits on whom he would stick his dick into. He even fucked his own cousin.

"Tracey…it's not Milli, it's Ginger."

She laughed and said, "So you finally got the guts to call me? Well I'm glad you did because I'm tired of these games. And just so you know, I plan to raise Denise with my husband."

"Your husband? What are you talking about? Milli never told me you had a husband."

"Milli lied to you and me about a lot of things, Ginger. I'm not Milli's cousin, I'm his wife. He told me you were his baby's mother, who he fucked on the side, and now I'm finding out you two have a relationship. It's cool though, because I'll hold him down always."

I was so angry I was trembling. I realized that I didn't know shit about Milli and felt like shooting him again. He was a complete stranger to me.

"You know what, it doesn't even matter anymore. I gave Milli something to hold for me close to his heart. You'll find out what it is later." I laughed. "I'm on my way to pick up my baby from you. Have her ready when I get there."

I hung up, grabbed my purse and dug into Milli's pockets for money. His eyes were closed but I knew he was still alive, he'd be dead soon though. Once I walked outside and took all of the money out of his Range Rover, I was fifteen thousand dollars richer. There was no turning back and I was officially on the run. I know his uncle Kettle's gonna kill me when he finds out that I killed Milli. The thing is, he has to find me first.

CHAPTER 10

GERRON

I knocked on the door of a run down house up the street from my block. Bodie rented a room from this crack head and paid her by the day. I guess they were getting high together because when he wasn't with me he was with her. This dude fell way off.

"Who you?" A little kid asked opening the door to greet me. He scratched at his ashy knees.

"Is, Bodie here?"

"Yeah," he said with an attitude. "Wait out here for a second. My mommy don't like company when her titties hanging out and she in the living room." He said slamming the door in my face.

Bodie came out five minutes later and I smelled crack in the air. I knew this nigga was getting high. I'm so glad I'm disassociating with this dude. He could've gotten me killed.

"What you want?" he asked me with low lids. "I thought you was gone." He leaned against the doorway and crossed his arms over his chest.

"Here," I said throwing the bag of dope at him. "I hit Milli. Now you ain't got no reason to fuck with Ginger."

His eyes widened and he picked the bag up, opened it and smiled. "Damn, you really are feeling this broad ain't you?"

"You got what you wanted, Bodie. And just so you know, me and you ain't got no more business."

He frowned. "So it's like that now? You come drop a bag of dope on my steps and then tell me we through?"

I turned my back on him and jumped in my car.

He was no longer worthy of an answer.

CHAPTER 11

GINGER

I banged heavily on Stevie's weak ass wooden door, stepped back and waited for her to come out. Before I go get my daughter, I wanted to address them to their face about fucking my man. I remember everything now and I wanted her to know.

"Bitch, you must be crazy knocking on my door like that," Stevie said walking toward the door. I could see kids inside her house everywhere running around, but I didn't see Melissa.

The moment she opened the door I laid into her. "So you fucked my man, Stevie? Is no dick off limits around you?"

She laughed and said, "So he finally told your dumb ass, huh? I didn't think he ever would." She folded her arms against her chest. "I gotta start giving Milli more credit."

You not going to be giving Milli shit. The nigga's dead.

I frowned and said, "All of your kids, Stevie? My man is the father to every one of your children?"

She laughed and I grew angrier.

"Nicky knows those his kids too?" I asked.

"What do you think, Ginger? Are you that stupid? The only one who was left out of the loop was you."

"That's why Nicky wanted me to dump him? So ya'll could have him?"

She shrugged and I felt flushed, embarrassed and hurt. And then Melissa, her daughter, walked behind Stevie and out onto the porch. "Get your little nosey ass in the house, Melli! That's your problem now, always being sneaky and listening to other people's conversations."

Stevie slapped her so hard in the face, her skin reddened immediately. Melli looked horrified when she saw me. I don't know if it was because Stevie hit her or if it was something else. When I looked closer at her, into her eyes, I believed I knew what her fear was. Melli was wondering if I was going to tell that she was the one who told me that Milli was her father. As angry as I was, I wasn't going to put a little girl out there like that. I knew then that Stevie did not put her up to calling me, so who did?

"Take your funky ass into the house," Stevie continued. "Now!"

Melli ran inside and I looked at Stevie. "You a stand up fucking mother. A real gem. Sit up there and hit that little girl for nothing."

"You should talk," she laughed. "Where is your daughter again? Oh I remember, in the custody of Child Protective Services."

Silence.

"So let me ask you something, when dude robbed us earlier you had something to do with setting your own cousin up today?" I asked.

"Setting my cousin up?" Stevie laughed. "Bitch we was setting you up! That entire robbery was to hit your head. Nicky told me somebody told you about the robbery, what I want to know is who?"

I knew then that Melli must've been overhearing her mother's conversation like she said when she called me. Wow!

"He was gonna come in that bitch and rob you, and take the rest of your jewelry too, but Gerron bitch ass mixed in. It was cool though, because we got all our money back after we met up with Treasure later."

"But Nicky came to my house about the robbery and acted like she was mad at me. Saying Gerron may be involved and all of that shit."

"That was all in our plan to throw your ass off. At the end of the day we want your ass gone, Ginger. Don't you get it? People keep telling you that but you not listening. It's so bad that even your man is involved. It was Milli who set the fight up for Trixy to step to you earlier today. He even knew about the robbery. All of this shit was his doing."

Who had I been with all of this time? Half of the shit Milli did to me, he didn't have to. He could've made me leave but he kept making it like it was my choice.

I'm so sick of this shit. Since I already had two bodies on my belt what would one more hurt? "You know what, fuck Milli and fuck you and Nicky too," I said digging in my purse for my gun.

I was about to commit murder for the third time in my life when I saw Stevie look behind me and smile. When I turned my head to see what caught her I was staring at Trixy and Shonda. Trixy hit me with an iron baseball bat on my shoulders and I fell face first. Trixy and Shonda kicked and punched me multiple times all over my body. I wanted to scream but my voice felt trapped inside of my gut.

"Now what, bitch?" Trixy said. "I told you earlier that before the night was over you would see my ass again! You thought it was a game."

"Yeah, you ain't got so much mouth now do you?" Shonda asked kicking me in my stomach.

"What are you doing, Stevie?" Nicky said rushing out of Stevie's house. "Are you tripping? Why ya'll got this girl out here in front of the house like that?"

When I looked up I saw my bracelet on her arm. What a fucking low down snake. But since she seemed mad I was hopeful that Nicky was gonna put an end to this shit. If we were ever friends this would prove it.

"The bitch came over here starting shit," Stevie yelled. "I ain't 'bout to let her jump in my face. So I handled her right here."

Nicky looked at me with compassion in her eyes. Then she looked at Stevie and said, "You know what you gotta do. We can't have no more police 'round here asking questions."

Stevie smiled and said, "Y'all heard my cousin. Kill the bitch."

CHAPTER 12

GERRON
THE NEXT DAY

Last night, when I was leaving the neighborhood for good, I saw Stevie and them punishing Ginger on the sidewalk. I jumped out, scooped her up and put her in my car. Stevie tried to step to me and I ended up smacking her with the back of my hand and rolling out. I guess I ended up hitting a female after all.

I know I should've taken Ginger to the hospital, but too much shit was going on and I ain't think she would be safe there. I did all I could to take care of her, but I had a feeling she wouldn't make it. Ginger hadn't opened her eyes since I helped her get away from Stevie's house.

Maybe it was a good thing that she wasn't conscious. This morning I found out from some people that Ginger tried to kill Milli and failed. He was in intensive care but stable. She should have shot the nigga in the head, and now he was gunning for her and me too.

Of course I missed my flight to Las Vegas so I decided we'd stay in a remote hotel in Virginia surrounded by trees and peace until she got better. Nobody would ever find us here, at least I hoped. I just wanted shawty to pull through otherwise this would be all for nothing.

It was ten o'clock at night and I was rolling a blunt when Ginger finally opened her eyes. I put the jay down and rushed to her side. "Take it easy, Ginger. You fucked up."

"Where...where am I?" She said in a low voice touching her head.

"You with me," I smiled. "So you safe for now. But how you feeling?"

"I have a bad ass headache," she smiled. "So you came back for me after all. I thought them bitches were going to kill me."

"I came back for you but we got a problem," I paused. "Ginger, why you ain't shoot them peoples in the head if you were trying to kill him? He's alive."

She sighed and said, "Damn." She looked away from me. I could tell she understood the severity of the situation.

"What were you thinking?"

"I thought I did kill him." she paused. "On another note I remember everything about that night. That I lost my memory. You were trying to stop me from going inside, because you knew they were in the house wasn't you?"

"Yeah."

"All this time I thought you were protecting them, and you were protecting me. You didn't want my feelings to get hurt. I'm so sorry, Gerron. I blamed you for nothing."

"Don't worry 'bout that."

"You know I can't go back and I can never be with my daughter," she cried.

"That ain't true," I responded. "You could turn yourself in, and maybe the charges won't be so bad."

I was talking bullshit and she knew it.

"I committed murder, Gerron. It's over. It's just a matter of time before Milli wakes up and tells the cops that I killed my best friend."

I wanted to offer her hope, when my phone rang. "Hello."

"Baby, can you hear me?" The sound of my mother's shaken voice had me on edge.

"Ma," I hopped up and paced the room. "You okay? Why you sound like that?"

"It's Bodie," she whispered. "He...he says he's gonna kill me, unless you can give him one hundred thousand dollars. Son, I don't want to die."

CHAPTER 13

STEVIE'S HOUSE

It was two in the morning when Melli snuck into her big sister Crystal's bedroom and slammed the door shut.

"I did what you ask me to," Melli whispered. "I called Ginger and told her Milli was my father. Now you gotta give me my stuff."

Crystal never believed her sister would do what she dared her but she was wrong. Melli had proven to be a baby gangster. Crystal, with her jealous heart, hated the way Milli doted over Denise, Ginger's daughter. More than anything she hated the way Ginger looked down at her.

So a few days earlier when she heard her mother and aunt plotting to rob Ginger, she came up with the plan to tell Ginger the truth about Milli in the hopes of ruining Ginger's life. She wasn't concerned with getting caught because she'd blame the whole thing on nosey Melli if her mother Stevie ever found out.

"Let me give you your stuff so you can get out of my face," Crystal said with an attitude.

Crystal pulled a shoebox from under her bed and handed Melli four packs of nacho cheese sunflower seeds and a pickled sausage. With her reward in hand Melli plopped happily on the edge of the bed and started eating.

As Melli chewed her snack, Crystal watched her. She wondered if Melli could be bribed with something so small, what else would she be willing to do if the prize were slightly bigger. The worst part is that she had all intentions on finding out.

CHAPTER 14

ONE YEAR LATER

*A strong odor of gasoline and gunpowder perme-
ated the car as Ginger sped down the road. Her left
hand clenched the steering wheel as she struggled to
control the large SUV. When she looked to her right she
focused on Gerron's eyes. Although he appeared to be
staring in her direction, she couldn't tell if life existed
behind them or not. Was he dead? Was he alive? Could
she save him?*

*Her eyes rolled onto the bullet hole in his chest
from the gunshot he sustained earlier. The bullet ripped
into the fabric of his white t-shirt, turning it into a circle
of red blood. He didn't look good at all.*

*"I'm gonna get you out of here, Gerron," she said
looking at him and then the road. "Just don't fucking die
on me. I can't be—"*

*Ginger's thought was broken when a hot slug
crashed into the back window of the truck, and tore into
the flesh of her left hand. The killers wanted her dead,
and they were willing to do anything to see that it happened. This was the worst-case scenario.*

"Leave me alone," she screamed looking at the two black SUV's in her rearview mirror. "Just leave us alone!"

Although her only functional hand was now injured, Ginger did all she could to maintain control of the vehicle. She lost so much already, and didn't want to lose Gerron too. But when another bullet tore into her right arm all hope was lost. That meant both her left and right arms were out of order.

Since she could no longer drive with her hands, Ginger raised her leg up and tried steering the truck with her knee. But the truck was moving fifty miles per hour and was pushing toward the huge tractor-trailer truck parked to the right.

Danger was imminent.

CHAPTER 15

GINGER
SIX MONTHS EARLIER
LAS VEGAS, NEVADA

Air rushed under the tight red dress I wore and brushed against my sweaty pussy. I took a shower not even five minutes ago yet I was still nervous. There's something about violence that arouses and scares me at the same time. Had me wanting to fuck. Maybe I'm going mad.

I took a deep breath and I approached the handsome Vegas Whale who was sitting in the High Rollers lounge with a beautiful black woman. This was my first time approaching a couple, which was Gerron's idea, and I hoped it worked. We always went at one prey at a time but this was different. This had to work. Things were set into motion and there was no turning back.

As I swaggered toward my prey, the only things in my hands are the rock glass filled with Hedonism Whiskey and my small gold purse. I tucked my purse under my armpit, and smoothed my 1960's-styled bun with my hand and readied myself for ACT ONE.

My prey looked to be of either Pakistani or Indian descent. I couldn't be sure, and it wasn't even like it mattered. I was interested in the green inside of his bank, and not the color of his skin tone. Although my target was sitting down in the chocolate leather chair, by the way his legs rested under his body, I could tell he was extremely tall. The blue designer slacks he was wearing did nothing to hide the dick print swelling between his legs. The beautiful black woman on his arm, who was probably a model, hit the jackpot when she landed his ass.

When I reached them I sat at the leather chair in front of them. A small glass table sat in the middle of us and I placed my purse and whiskey upon it, all without saying a word to the couple. I used this moment to speak to my prey with my eyes as I crossed my legs and smiled.

"Winning?" I finally asked him.

He smirked slyly, in a way that only a millionaire could. "Always."

I nodded and observed the diamond engagement ring on his lady's finger. By this time she's looking at me as if she wants to kill me.

"You're very beautiful," I told her running my tongue over my red lips, as if I tasted her. "Stunning even."

Before the compliment she was glaring at me like she wanted to rip out my throat, but now she was twinkling. I learned a lot during the time I'd been with Gerron. He's an excellent teacher. He taught me that diamonds and money will always be a woman's best friend, but the one thing she desires more in life, more than anything, is to be noticed.

"I appreciate the compliment," she responded before pulling her thick brown hair behind her ear. She looked over my shoulder at the tables. "Do you play?"

"I play very well," I responded in a seductive tone. She blushed.

I got her right where I wanted her and it wasn't even hard.

"I'm talking about the games," she grinned. "Do you play the games?"

"No, but my husband Oba does," I responded nodding at Gerron who was at the poker table. "I leave those types of things to him."

The three of us looked over at Gerron who was focused on the game. He was playing the part and he was doing well too. He had stacks of chips in front of him and a look of confidence on his face. For us to be from the hood we sure knew how to clean up and our victims were never the wiser. We both played The Game well.

"Is he winning?" her man asked me.

"Everything he touches prospers."

About twenty minutes later Gerron walked over to us. The fresh haircut he got earlier, and the black and gray pinstripe suit he sported made him look heavy. Money heavy. Damn he was turning me on! Although I wanted to take it one step further with Gerron, by being husband and wife, I got the impression that he wasn't ready for the next step. I do know something though. After the way Milli did me, I wasn't going to be playing house with this nigga for the rest of my life. He was either going to make me the one, or leave me alone.

Gerron walked behind me, placed his hands on my shoulders and kissed me on my earlobe. My pussy jumped and I knew he did that shit on purpose. He knew my spot. He knew all of my spots. Gerron made it his business to know everything about me, and that's why I fucking loved him.

My baby sat next to me, his arm brushed softly against mine, while the Vegas Whale sat on the other side.

"Oba," I said referring to Gerron, "this is Hassan." They shook hands and the room appeared to rock. I love power. "And this is his beautiful fiancé Chloe." Gerron nodded toward her and she grinned.

"It's a pleasure," he said to her.

"So Oba, what do you do?" Hassan asked.

"Films," Gerron responded after sipping the whiskey placed in front of him recently by the waiter. He stirred the ice in his glass with a soft shake of his wrist, which caused the diamond watch on his arm to sparkle. We spent a lot of money for our costumes, to look the part. A lot of money.

"Is that right," Hassan said sarcastically. "Have I seen any of them?"

Gerron shrugged. "Most of my films are made in my hometown Nigeria so you probably have not. They call the projects completed there, *Nollywood* movies as opposed to Hollywood. But no matter what they call them, they have made me a very rich man."

Hassan raised his rock glass and we all followed. "To riches," Hassan nodded.

"To kings," Gerron replied.

Before long Gerron and Hassan tossed around poker lingo while his fiancé Chloe and me eye fucked each other. Things were heating up really quickly when another part of our plan kicked into action. I dug into my purse and grabbed my phone to prepare.

As Gerron and I held fake court with the High Roller, Carson, a tall white man who had been on our payroll since we'd first arrived to Vegas six months ago, walked up to us.

"Oh my, is that you, Oba," Carson asked stopping next to our seats. He had a beautiful red head on his arm whose smile was as wide as Chloe's legs were at the moment. Did I also forget to mention that she wasn't wearing panties? That pussy was exposed and I loved it.

Gerron stood up and shook Carson's hand firmly. "Yes, and you are?"

"You don't know me, but I wrote a review for a few of your movies recently for the New York Times. That was before the Oscar nod you got for Best Independent Film of course. Congratulations. You deserve it."

"Thanks, man," Gerron responded. He looked down at Hassan. "Oh, before I forget this is"— Gerron placed both hands on Hassan's shoulders and bent down close to Hassan's ear— "save me, man, what is your name again?"

Hassan grinned and whispered, "Hassan."

Gerron patted him on the back hard. "This is Hassan. Join us for a drink."

Carson shook Hassan's hand and said, "I really can't. I just wanted to tell you congratulations. You own the industry now, and you deserve it. "

Gerron dapped him up. "Thanks, man."

Carson and his beauty walked out of the scene leaving the four of us alone.

I saw the smile on Gerron's face when Carson left because everything was going as planned. Gerron knows people. I'm not talking about the basic characteristics needed to know if a person is nice, vile or weak. He really knows people. He knows their souls. And although he kept a gun on him most of the time, he never had to use it. Well, he didn't have to pull the trigger anyway.

Before long the expensive drinks were flowing and I was feeling good. It looked like all of us were. What I learned about rich people over this year was that they bored easily, which always led to trouble. It made them easy to fall victims to people like us because they craved excitement. You can listen to so many stock stories from your friends before you lost your mind. That's where we came in. The young. The exciting. The rich.

For a moment I sat back and watched Gerron and Hassan talk about Poker and Blackjack. So I stood up and walked over to Chloe.

Looking down at our men I said, "What are we going to do with these men and their games?" I placed my hand on her shoulder and moved one finger along her warm skin so that it was out of view from everybody else.

She looked up at me. "I don't know maybe we can play some games of our own."

"That sounds good to me."

CHAPTER 16

GINGER

The hotel room was pitch black and I was lying in between Chloe's hot legs while kissing her plush lips. Her warm tongue wiggled inside of my mouth while I jerked Hassan's big dick off. I could taste the alcohol in her mouth and her nails traced down my back, causing me to shiver. I wasn't into girls per say, but I had to admit, this was nice.

"Let me feel inside of you," Hassan begged looking over at us tease him. We had been at it for five minutes and I guess he was starting to get bored. "I can't take it any more."

I removed my lips from Chloe's and looked over at him. "Be patient, sweetheart. I'm coming over there in a minute. I'm just warming up your fiancé a little bit that's all."

As I continued to kiss her I could feel Hassan growing increasingly annoyed. His dick was getting softer in my palm and I wondered what the fuck was Gerron doing. He told us that he was going to get in the shower, and would join us in a minute but I needed him now. This dude was becoming a hand full.

"Okay, that's enough kissing my fiancé," Hassan said with a heavy voice. "Get over here now. I want to feel inside of you."

Not wanting to mess up the plan I eased over toward him. He yanked me by the back of my neck and roughly stuffed his tongue into my mouth. He moved his tongue back and forth over mine, causing thick long strings of spit to hang from the corners of my mouth. "Fucking, nigger. How long do you think I was going to sit idly by and let you tell me what you wanted to do? Do you know who I am? A fucking king! I pick up cheap bitches like you at lower spots. You aren't running anything."

I was horrified in that moment. Gerron and I pulled these types of jobs all the time, but this was the first time we went after couples. Normally I would seduce the man, lead him up to my room, and then walk him to the bank to take some money out. We would threaten to hurt his family and that seemed to work for a while. But the last dude we hit, ended up getting away from us when we tried to get the money. We figured if we grabbed couples instead, and hold one hostage while the other goes to the bank, they would have more to lose. I hoped this shit worked.

"Wait a minute, baby," I said trying not to focus on the fact that he called me a nigger. I really wanted to flip on his ass. "You don't have to be so rough with me. I want to play too. All you gotta do is be easy."

"Ain't no being easy. What type of games are you playing huh?" he asked as he tried to push my pussy onto his stiff dick. "I came up here for a reason." Instead of falling onto his stick I pushed upward but it was getting hard. "I want to get into you before your husband gets out of the shower and ruins our fun."

"But my husband is with it, Hassan," I smiled hoping to calm him down. "He wants to play with Chloe a little too. Remember? There's no rush...you know that."

"Hassan, she's right, sweetheart," Chloe said nervously. Her words were broken and she didn't sound as confident as she did earlier in the night. "We're just going to have a little fun tonight. No reason to rush or be so rough."

I was hopeful he would listen to her instead he stuffed his finger into my asshole. He pulled it out and wiped it across my upper lip. I could smell my own feces.

"Um...I love chocolate pudding." He licked it off.

I was humiliated until he grabbed my neck and started squeezing. I tried to fight him but he had a good hold of me. The more he crushed my windpipe the lower my waist went until I could feel his stiffness press against the opening of my pussy. I knew either he was about to rape or kill me, neither of which was in the plan.

I said a silent prayer and made my peace with the world until I heard Chloe gasp for air, followed by the click of a gun. When I looked to my right I saw Gerron standing behind Chloe, with a muscled forearm around her neck, while his gun was aimed at Hassan.

Hassan released my neck and slowly air rushed back into my lungs. I rolled off of him and rubbed my sore throat. When I was done I punched Hassan over and over in the face, until my knuckles cracked against his cheeks. I didn't stop until my arms felt weak.

Gerron laughed and said, "That's enough, babe. I got it from here."

I slapped Hassan one more time and paced the floor next to the bed. Since I got with Gerron I tuned my temper all the way down. I didn't want to lose him like I felt I lost Milli, because of my so-called attitude problem. But this shit took me way over the edge and if I had my gun next to me I would've killed him.

"Can somebody tell me what the fuck is going on here?" Hassan asked as he sat up in the bed and leaned his head against the headboard. He rubbed his face.

"You mean outside of the fact that you were just choking my bitch?" Gerron responded with Chloe's neck still under his hold.

"Yes!"

"Let me put it this way. I have good news and bad news." Gerron placed a strand of Chloe's hair behind her ear with the barrel of the gun. "Which one do you want first, my man?"

Hassan wiped his thick black hair backwards and sighed. "The bad."

"Okay, here it is. You going to be fifty thousand dollars lighter this evening."

Hassan leaned his head toward Gerron, widened his eyes and burst into laughter. "Is that all this is about? Fifty fucking thousand dollars? Are you serious? Do you have any idea how much I'm worth? Any idea at all?"

"Why don't you tell me?"

"A lot! I'm worth millions!"

Gerron laughed. "Is that right?"

"That's fucking right! And you niggers have no idea who you're fucking with. None! If you had any clue you would tuck tail and run while you still have the chance."

"Thanks for enlightening us on your financial status," I said with a smile. "What do you think, Oba? Did we hold our price a little too low?"

"We held our price way too low if you ask me."

"What should we do about that," I asked with my hands on my hips. My messy bun hanging to the left.

Gerron looked at Hassan. "The new price is one hundred thousand dollars."

"Cash," I added.

Hassan lowered his head, and then slammed it into the headboard. When he looked back up his eyes told me that he wanted to kill us. "So I guess you're not a filmmaker."

"Oh I'm a filmmaker alright." Gerron looked over at me. "Queue the video, baby so this nigga can see my work."

I rushed to my cell phone that was on the dresser. I scanned the videos of our other victims and played the one with me jerking his dick while I slobbed his fiancé down. They didn't know that Gerron was hanging in the corner with the night vision on while we did our thing. When I was done I showed the video I took of Gerron bending next to Hassan's ear earlier in the evening. The way I positioned the camera it looked as if Gerron had kissed him instead of whispered in his ear. All of the video was taken to look like one thing— that we were all swingers. Although we had nothing to lose, we knew that a huge businessman like Hassan did.

"Right now the video doesn't look like much, but when it's put together, using my movie making skills of course," Gerron said sarcastically, "it will look like the four of us participated in a foursome, and that includes me and you too." He said waving the gun back and forth between them. "Also what they'll see, and you're lucky I don't break your neck for this part, is how you tried to rape my woman when she refused to fuck you. You don't want this shit going viral on the Internet now do you?"

Hassan's dark skin tone reddened. "Fuck, you niggers. You have no idea the shit—"

"Shut the fuck up, Hassan," Chloe screamed startling me. "I'm so sick of your fucking mouth! You have gotten us in enough trouble as is, and if I tell my father how you continue to disrespect me and my heritage; he'll pull out of that investment deal next month! Now you may be well off, but that deal has the potential to make you more money than Bill Gates."

Gerron and I busted out laughing.

"Damn, main man," Gerron said, "I guess you not the money maker you thought you were huh?" Gerron got serious. "Fuck all that though. Get dressed, slim, we going downstairs. It's time to see what a nigga of your caliber is really working with."

CHAPTER 17

GERRON

Luckily the place was basically empty as I stood close to Hassan inside of the Bank of Nevada. It was unusually close and it made me feel gay. But I needed him to know that if he made the slightest move, I wouldn't hesitate to load him with lead using the gun stuffed in my pocket.

I hoped it wouldn't be too much longer. He already told the attendant how much cash he wanted to withdraw, and it didn't seem to be a big deal. It was obvious that everyone in here knew him, and he was a regular.

When a female bank attendant, followed by an armed guard, brought the money back over to Hassan in a black briefcase, he shook her hand firmly and we both left the bank. Together.

This was the first time we pulled off the couple thing and it looked like everything was going smoothly. When we made it to Hassan's gray Lincoln sedan out front, I had him drive us back to the hotel, while I held my barrel aimed at his waist in case he got weird again.

I still wasn't over him trying to rape Ginger, but I would make him pay for it later.

"I looked up your picture on the internet, when you told me you were a filmmaker," he said to me.

"When you do all that?"

"When we were in the casino."

"So," I responded ready to blow his intestines out if he made a move.

"So everything you said, with you being a filmmaker looked true. How did you pull that off?"

I laughed and shook my head. "People give the internet too much credit."

"What does that mean?" he frowned driving slower than I wanted him too.

"First of all pick up the speed a little. We not cruising, nigga. This is a business ride." He drove faster but not above the driving limit. "As far as the Internet answer me this, which media outlet holds the most power in the world right now?"

Hassan shrugged. "What do you mean?"

"You a millionaire," I said, "or so you claim to be, and you can't answer that question?"

He looked over at me with irritation and then back at the road. "You saw how they treated me in that bank just now with your own eyes. They didn't even flinch when I withdrew a hundred thousand dollars. So trust me, I am who I say I am." He focused back on the highway. "Anyway I know stocks and bonds, not media outlets. My favorite paper is the Wall Street Journal, beyond that I don't care about much else."

I laughed. "Let me school you. The most powerful media outlets are the blogs. For the right money you can pay anybody to blog about anything that you want. You approach enough bloggers, and have them write about you and that's when the magic begins. If you do it enough when somebody such as yourself asks for a name, a simple Internet search will pull up what you want to show people. In the end you can control what the world reads about you."

Hassan laughed. "So you created this Oba personality just to extort money?"

I smiled. "It's a lucrative business."

He exhaled and gripped the steering wheel harder. I could tell because his knuckles whitened. "What's your real name?"

Silence.

"I get it, I get it," he nodded again. "You don't want to tell me your real name. I might not like you but I will say this, you're smarter than I gave you credit for."

"Most people underestimate me, although they shouldn't. All of them regret it later."

"I get that, but a smart man such as yourself should also know that you can't have a career like this for the rest of your life. At some point you are going to need a big hit, which will afford you the opportunity to get out of the business for good."

I focused on his eyes. "What exactly are you trying to say?"

"I have something you might be interested in." His eyelids lowered making him look demonic. "Something that will give you enough money to take care of yourself and that pretty little woman of yours for life."

"I already got your money," I said nodding to the back seat. "Haven't you been paying attention?"

He laughed. "I'm paying attention but you're not listening. The opportunity I'm trying to give you will net you a million dollars." he focused on the road. "Are you interested now?"

I looked at the shiny red Maserati that was weaving in and out of traffic in front of me. I use to want a car like that, until I realized they brought with them unwanted attention from the FEDS. With the schemes Ginger and I were running, we saved almost half a million dollars, before we bought our house. Although the original money needed to pay the ransom, and get my mother back from Bodie, was only one hundred grand, due to circumstances beyond my control I never got the chance to get her back.

When I called and told him I had the money, I found out he got locked up when the house he lived in was involved in a raid. Nobody knew where my mother was, so I had to wait for him to come home from jail in another month to find out. A million dollars would come in handy right now for sure.

"What's the plan?" I asked Hassan.

"Chloe is a really beautiful woman isn't she?" he asked skipping the subject.

I shrugged. "Your point?"

"I'm going to marry her and make her my wife. In the *beginning* I'm going to make her a very happy woman."

"The beginning?"

He looked at me seriously. It was as if time stopped and it caused me to cock my gun. "I want her murdered six months into our marriage. That will give me enough time to let this deal go through with her father." He looked over at me. "I'm not a criminal, but you are. So what do you think?"

"I think you a snake ass nigga."

"This from a man who's extorting me," he laughed.

"This from the nigga who can shatter your ribs with the tug of my trigger finger," I said stabbing the barrel into his waist for a firm reminder.

He flinched. "Easy," he responded in a slow voice. "I didn't mean to disrespect you. I just figured since you are robbing me that you would be interested in a bigger payout that's all."

"Let me tell you something 'bout me. I'm a stick up dude. I take worthless pieces of shit like you to the bank and tax you hard. Consider it a luxury tax. But I'm not a murderer. I don't pull my gun unless I have to or want to."

"So you never fired your gun before?" he asked with malice in his eyes. As if he could take me now because I didn't have that much experience.

"You wanna try me?"

Silence.

"It's funny," he said in a low voice as we pulled up to the hotel.

"What's that?"

"I guess what I've heard all this time is a lie. There really must be honor amongst thieves."

CHAPTER 18

GERRON

I can't lie I love this bitch. I know she hates when I call her that shit, but it's the truth. We at this restaurant, a real slick one with dark lights and shit like that. I told her we needed to dress up and she did a good job. She wore a black piece that hugs her waist and cuts high on the side. Since the first day I met her, Ginger was the sexiest bitch I ever met, and now she's about to be mine.

Tonight I'm going to ask her the big question, and I feel confident about her reply. I know she want a nigga to propose. She's always bringing it up slyly.

I rubbed my pocket and was about to take the ring out until she said, "Why did you whisper in Chloe's ear? Right before she left with Hassan?"

"I told her to watch her back, and that her nigga offered me a million dollars to take her life. I told her that since I didn't do it I'm sure somebody else was going to do the job, and that she'd better be careful."

She looked down at her garlic spinach. "Gerron, why did you wait so long to come into the room when Hassan was choking me?" she scooped some food into

130

her mouth. "I'm not understanding your reaction time. It was off at best."

I took my hand off of my pocket and grabbed my glass of whiskey instead. "What you talking about, ma?" I took a large sip and put it down on the table.

"When we did the job the other day. With Hassan and Chloe. How come you waited so long to help me? The nigga almost killed me."

"Ginger, I couldn't see from where I was standing that he was choking you. You know I wouldn't have left you out there like that. The fact that you would even think that makes me feel like you don't know what you mean to me. Like I'm less than a man."

"But he was calling me a nigger and everything, G. I mean what the fuck? I thought he was gonna rape me and shit."

"So you sitting over there thinking that I would do that to you on purpose?" I felt my vein pulsing in my head. I do everything for this bitch, and she still don't know how I feel about her. "You really think that I would have some mothafucka choking you and not do nothing about it? That's what you think of me?"

"All I'm saying is that it looked suspect."

"Then tell me why his eye was swollen when he came back into the room."

"I thought he fell or something?"

"Yeah, on my fist, Ginger. I couldn't do to him what I wanted before we left because I needed his face alright when we went to the bank. I didn't want people being suspicious in there and not give us the money. But he paid for putting his hands on you. What is it with you, Ginger?"

"What kind of question is that?"

"A clear one. What the fuck is up with you? Why is it that no matter how close I try to get to you, you constantly push me back? Do you want an enemy in me or a man?"

She rolled her eyes. "I'm not trying to push you back I was just asking a question. I mean if..."

She was saying something else but I couldn't hear her. "Speak up, Ginger. Fuck you saying under your breath over there? Why is nothing ever good enough for you?"

"I want to see my daughter, Gerron," she said softly. "When the fuck are we gonna do that?"

I sat back in my seat. "I know you ain't trying to blame me as the reason you haven't seen Denise. What happened four months ago when we tried to get her from Milli's wife?"

"I'm not talking about —"

"What the fuck happen?" I yelled.

Ginger looked around her at the people who were looking our way. Then she looked into my eyes. "The police were there"— she pushed a strand of her long hair behind her ears— "because somebody told Tracey I was in town and was coming to get my kid."

I leaned closer to the table. "And what did I tell you even with the cops out there?"

She cleared her throat. "That you didn't care about the cops. And that you would go up in that bitch and get Denise if I wanted you to."

"I told you to give me the word and it was done. And what did you tell me?"

"That I wanted to do it in a different way, because I didn't want to lose you too."

I sat back again and exhaled. I didn't want to go at her so hard but Ginger moves like a dude sometimes. She's swift with her mouth and she gets mad when you say something she don't like. The fucked up part is that I still love her. Probably always will. I can't get her out of my mind even though I should. I knew she was the one for me since we was neighbors in Kentland. But if she don't change we'll have to go our separate ways.

"I know you want to be with your kid, Ginger. You know I do. But you gotta make the call on what you're willing to risk. On what you're willing to give up. I can't do that for you. Whatever call you make, you can't blame me a couple months down the line if things don't go your way."

"I know that."

"If you know that then why you coming at me sideways?"

She placed her elbow on the table and put her face in her hands. "I don't know what to do. I'm so fucked up right now, Gerron. I feel like a worthless mother, but I don't know which move to make either." She looked up at me and I wanted to protect her, and make her feel safe. "I feel like we should've moved and got my daughter when Tracey was by herself, even with the cops being there. Because now Milli moved them somewhere private and I don't know where she is."

"It's like this, baby, there's no easy route in this scenario. I'm gonna be straight up. Either we gonna go back home and grab your kid and be ready to deal with the cops and Milli, or we let somebody you can't stand raise her. The biggest thing you gotta do is decide."

She sighed. "You know what the funny part about all of this is?"

"Naw."

"Back in the day I use to get mad at Milli when he made my decisions for me. You know? And now I realize he's what I needed all along."

Through clenched teeth I asked, "So you saying you miss your old nigga? That's what you telling me to my face? After everything I put on the line for you?"

"I'm telling you that a bitch, even a hood one like me, wants a man to take care of her every now and again."

That was it. I was officially done with Ginger. She don't deserve a nigga of my caliber and I definitely wasn't about to ask this bitch to be my wife. I stood up, dug in my pocket and slammed the ring box on the table.

"Thanks for saving me from making a mistake."

When she looked at it, and I could tell she knew what it was, I dipped off.

CHAPTER 19

GINGER

As I watched Gerron walk away, dressed in his designer gray slacks and gray shirt, I realized I made a huge mistake. Sometimes I speak out of anger because I'm frustrated with how slow things are moving in my life right now. It may be a little boredom too.

After we raised the ransom for Gerron's mother, and Bodie got locked up, I complained that I missed the rich life I was accustomed to. So he thought up this scheme we did of robbing people for large sums of money instead of small change. With the paper we had we were able to buy a beautiful home in Nevada, and I had more clothes and jewelry than my eyes could see. With everything I have, I'm still sad. How can I be anything but? My daughter is not with me, I don't know if the cops are looking for me for Leona's murder, and I love Gerron but feel bad about being with him.

I know it sounds wrong, and that I shouldn't be ashamed for loving Gerron, but I spent most of my life in love with one man—Terrod 'Milli' Knox. And without him I feel like I'm a different person. I feel like I'm cheating on him even though he slept with both of my best friends, which caused me to shoot my closest friend to death when I caught them fucking in our own house.

All I could think about was what I didn't have, not realizing I was losing a man I really did care about in the process. Gerron is not perfect, but he loves me and I think I fucked all of that up just now by shitting on his proposal.

He was going to ask me to be his wife, something I wanted, and I thought he didn't care.

I stood up from the table grabbed my phone out of my purse and walked over to the large window within the restaurant. I focused on the rain coming down outside and was immediately sadder. I took a deep breath and dialed his number. Since neither of us could have a personalized voicemail the call went to an automated service.

"Gerron, I didn't know you were about to ask me...I mean...please call me." I looked outside at a girl walking arm and arm with her man, while he held a red umbrella over her head. I miss my baby already. "Please come back to the restaurant. Let's get some drinks and talk."

When he didn't answer, I went back to the table and ordered another round of whiskey. Don't ask me why I started drinking whiskey instead of Bacardi Limon, but I think it had something to do with the rich people I had been around since our time in Vegas. They were rubbing off on me. Maybe I was trying to be someone I wasn't.

As I sat alone I got curious. Although I didn't want to open the ring box, because I hoped Gerron would give me the chance to say yes the proper way, I couldn't help myself. So I picked up the red velvet box, turned the mouth in my direction and popped it open like a clam.

"Wow, someone did good," an older white woman said with a smile on her face. She was standing behind me looking at the ring. "You're a lucky woman." She walked off.

She was right. The diamond was so large it looked like a flashlight was shining into my face. I bit down on my bottom lip and could taste my own blood. The nigga went all out and I fucked it up. I closed the box and stuffed it inside of my purse. We never stayed mad at each other too long so I was hoping now was no different.

I pulled my cell out and called him again.

Please, Gerron, pick up the phone. I thought to myself.

It rung twice until it was finally answered. "Hello," a woman responded laughing. "Who am I speaking to?"

My heart felt as if it dropped and slammed against the floor. "Who the fuck is this?" I jumped up. "Why you answering my nigga's phone?"

She laughed but I didn't see anything funny. My heart was on the line. "No...who the fuck is this?" the woman asked with a slight accent. "I have the phone not you."

"Bitch, I'm his mothafucking wife!" *Well I was about to be until I fucked it up.* "And I need to know who you are and what you doing with Gerron's phone!"

Click.

"Hello," I yelled. "Hello!"

The bitch hung up and I felt my head spin. I tossed my phone into my purse. "Waiter, get the fuck over here," I screamed at him. "I need a drink quick." When I looked over and saw that he was moving slowly I got louder. "I said hurry the fuck up!"

When he finally came over to me he had an attitude. "Ma'am, you can't use language like that—"

"Don't tell me what the fuck to use because I got money." I dug in my purse and tossed a hundred dollars on the table. "That's your tip which means I can talk to you any way I want too. I own you for the night. Remember that shit."

He smiled and suddenly was no longer upset. I bought him for a hundred dollars, but why did I feel like shit?

"Just bring me over another glass of whiskey. Better yet, make it the entire bottle." He was about to walk away but I grabbed his arm softly. "I'm sorry...I'm just...I'm just having a bad day, that's all."

"No problem," he said still grinning at his tip. "Let me grab your drink."

When he left I could feel myself about to cry again when I thought about that bitch answering the phone. Gerron was no better than Milli. He was all about pussy and he didn't care how I was feeling. The moment we get into an argument Gerron replaces me with some Spanish bitch he probably just met on the street? Just like that? I feel like unleashing in here. I feel like hurting somebody, and I also feel like fucking.

Whenever I get angry I feel the need to have sex, which is how me and Gerron got together in the first place. When I realized that my ex-boyfriend dumped me back then, I needed and escape and Gerron gave it to me in the form of a dick. I knew I was always attracted to him, but I gave myself a reason to be with him that day.

After five glasses of whiskey I felt my head spin. When a tall dude walked into the restaurant with three gold chains around his neck I wondered if I should revenge fuck him like Gerron did to me with that bitch who answered his phone.

Mr. Gold Chains wasn't even my type. He was too gaudy and I got the impression he wanted people to think he had money. Still, as he strutted over to the bar and leaned against it for the moment he had my attention.

So I flirted with him with my eyes, and he flirted back. When he smiled a little, and I saw his pearly white teeth my clit jumped. I was about to go over and introduce myself when he reached into his pocket and removed a stack of cash. Maybe I was wrong. Maybe he was sitting on a little paper after all. Suddenly fucking was the last thing on my mind. I wanted to rob his ass and I couldn't wait for Gerron to come back so that we could...

Wait.

Gerron and I just broke up.

Gerron was my right hand. My partner in crime. Without him on my side I couldn't do this shit. It wasn't just about our prey, it was also about the thrill we got when we hit people together.

Realizing I missed Gerron, I took my eyes off of Mr. Gold Chains. This was turning out to be the worst day of my life. When I turned around in my seat, and looked ahead of me Gerron was sitting at the table across from me like he never left. Like all of this was a bad dream.

"I don't know if you called, but I lost my phone."

I suppressed the smile I felt spreading on my cheeks. "You almost made me hurt you, Gerron. I'm serious."

"Now what I do?" he frowned.

"Some bitch answered your phone, and I thought you were fucking her or something."

"Is that right?" he grinned.

"Yes it is, and ain't shit funny either."

"So take it out on me in the bedroom," he said slyly. "Like we use to do."

I looked behind me, at Mr. Gold Chains. "Let's do it after."

"After what?" he asked.

"After we hit that bamma ass nigga over there at the bar." I nodded my head in Mr. Gold Chain's direction.

"You already know how much I love foreplay," he responded with a devilish grin on his face.

I was lying in the bed on Gerron's chest in our bedroom. Last night we hit the drug dealer hard which netted us a few thousand and a pound of weed that was inside of his car. It was chump change but that wasn't the point. It was so cool seeing Gerron's eyes light up as he stuck the gun in his face and told him to run them pockets. He was at home when he did that type shit. I knew then that although we extorted heavy weights in Vegas, for Gerron, there was no better feeling than re-lieving a drug dealer of his coins on the streets.

"So are you gonna ask me again?" I asked rubbing his chest.

He looked down at me. "Ask you what," he said running his hand down the middle of my back.

"To marry you."

He turned his head and closed his eyes.

"Gerron"— I looked up at him— "are you gonna ask me again or not, nigga?"

"I never asked you the first time remember? You shut that down." He pushed me off him softly, got out of the bed and walked toward the bathroom. I thought he was going to use the toilet but he closed the door and took a shower. Was he serious?

To relieve some of the pain I felt in my chest, I pulled the covers up to my chin and played with my pussy.

It only took me five minutes to drift off to sleep.
Fuck Gerron!

CHAPTER 20

GERRON

We were at the MGM Grand hotel on the strip and Ginger was drunk. I knew why she was doing this shit and it fucked me up. Why would she carry on like this when she knew we had work to do? Just because I wouldn't ask her to marry me.

She was standing by the bar, leaning forward like she was gonna fall on top of it. This shit was turning me off. "One more please," Ginger said to the bartender. "Make it quick too. I'm trying to get fucked up out here."

"She don't need another one," I said over her head. I put my hand on her back. "She's good."

She shook me off of her.

"Whatever you say," the bartender responded wiping his hands on a white hand towel and walking off.

She turned around and faced me. "Fuck is wrong with you," Ginger asked slurring. She could barely stand in the black expensive heels I bought her last week for this job. "You don't tell me what the fuck I can drink or how to drink it. Remember? You don't want to be my husband so don't say nothing else to me."

I shook my head. I knew she did this on purpose. "Well I told you anyway. You reached your limit so don't go over it anymore."

"But you not my fucking father, Gerron, you hear me? You not nothing to me, not even a man."

I pulled her toward me by her elbow. "First off why are you saying my name so fucking loud? We supposed to be scouting a job." I looked around us and luckily nobody was paying any attention to her show. "Fuck is wrong with you?"

She snatched away. "Why won't you propose to me, Gerron?" she placed her hand over her heart. "You don't want me nomore? If you don't I wish you'd be a man and say it to my face."

"You gotta be fucking kidding me," I walked to the far end of the bar and she followed me.

"Why you leaving? If...if...if you don't love me no more just answer the fucking question. Say it to my face at least."

"I would say it to your face but your breath stinks. Plus I'm not talking to you right now about no marriage shit. The last thing I want you to be is my wife."

Her eyes widened. "Well I guess I got my answer then"— she yanked my chin toward her— "you don't want me, and now I don't want you." Her warm breath was heavy with alcohol and if we were fucking my dick would go soft. "So go on, get the fuck out of my life.

I'm through with you anyway. I should've never left Kentland."

I was tempted to take her up on her offer, and leave her stranded in Vegas but she was my heart. "I want you to stop drinking, and I want you to come with me. We not gonna be able to do this job today. You had more than your share."

"Yes we are," she swayed. "We came to do it"— she stabbed a finger into the bar— "and we gonna do it."

"Ginger," I whispered heavily, "you not gonna be able to pull off the job like this. Do you understand?

"Well I'll do somebody else instead. You don't got the extortion gig on lock in Vegas. I don't need you."

Before I could snatch her out of here, a pretty girl approached us at the bar. "Please tell me ya'll didn't lose as much money as we did," she sat in one of the four available seats next to us. "I need to know somebody came out on top."

"Girl, we did alright," Ginger responded twirling the straw in her cup that I didn't even see the bartender give her, "but damn, them tables cold right now."

A dude in an eye patch sat behind the girl and rubbed her shoulder. I looked over at him, not knowing if I trusted him or not. Something felt off with the way he looked at me.

"The name is Swoopes," he said extending his hand to me. "And this is my girl Crystal."

He introduced himself so that was cool and all, but I still didn't know if I trusted them or not. My instincts kept me alive for a long time.

"And we are Ginger and Gerron," Ginger responded.

I knew she was drunk now. We never, EVER, gave out our names to people we planned to hit. Ginger was digging us deeper into shit and I didn't see this ending too well.

I was ready to call it quits but we ended up having a good conversation with them. I lied and told them we were from Atlanta and they told me they were from DC. The only other thing that didn't sit to well with me about this dude was the fact that three fingers were missing off of his right hand. I wondered what he did to lose most of his digits. Was he a thief like me and got caught up?

"What were ya'll playing?" Swoopes asked me.

"Blackjack. Nothing serious." I responded. "I told my baby to get the fuck up when she was winning but she didn't. Before I knew it she lost almost everything."

"*Almost* everything?" Swoopes repeated.

"Yep. I stopped her before she got too far."

"Why you put me out there, honey," Ginger said. "You was the main one handing me chips and shit."

"This girl crazy," I said, "she thinks just because chips are on the table you supposed to use 'em all. I told her you gotta quit while you still ahead."

Swoopes and Crystal laughed. "Well we have some vouchers for a nice restaurant at Bellagio's. If ya'll up for it we'd love the company," Crystal said.

"I don't know," Ginger said looking back at me. "We don't want to intrude."

"Come on," Crystal insisted with a smile on her face. "Drinks on us. You can't beat them odds."

Ginger looked at me and I said, "Fuck it. We ain't got nothing else to lose."

When we made it to the restaurant and popped a few bottles, I had to admit, we were having a good time. The longer I talked to both of them, the more I was reminded that they were from my hometown. Suddenly I had a new conspiracy theory. I think they were here for Bodie or Milli, so I was becoming uneasy. At the end of the day whatever we were going to do I wanted done so that we could hit them for the bread they claimed they made, and go 'bout our business.

So I said, "We got some drinks in our room. Ya'll wanna go back there and play cards or something?"

"We don't want to put you guys out," Crystal said to me.

"It's not a problem," Ginger replied, "It would be our pleasure."

"Sounds like a plan to me," Swoopes said giving me dap.

Within twenty minutes we were back in the hotel.

"We going to freshen up," Ginger said to them. "But we have some Berry and Coconut Ciroc on the table. Make yourselves at home."

"Thank you," Crystal said as she sat down.

When we walked into the bedroom I pulled Ginger closer so that only she could hear my voice. "You sure you ready to do this shit? We going way off the plan, baby. I don't know 'bout this. You had a lot to drink."

"I haven't had a drink since the first bar," she said to me. "I have a clear mind. Trust me."

"But you been tossing them up all night. I haven't seen you take a break."

"I been faking, Gerron. You were right about what you said at the bar. I played myself when it was time for business and I almost let you down. I was into my feelings and I'm never doing that again." She loaded her weapon and handed me mine. "So let's do this shit. I'm ready."

When we walked back into the living room we saw Swoopes moving for something in his waist. From where I stood I could tell he was strapped. They were about to hit us instead. This entire night was a set up on all of our parts.

"Don't move, baby boy," Ginger said loudly. She must've seen his gun too. "Get your mothafuckin' hands in the air." With her free hand she relieved them of their weapons.

"That's my bitch, nigga," I laughed. "That's how we do it!"

Ginger winked at me and looked back at Swoopes and Crystal.

"You know what time it is, nigga," I said with my gun planted on the back of his skull. "Give it up, 'fore I blow your other eye out from the back."

CHAPTER 21

GINGER

I stirred a little in our king size bed. When I looked over at Gerron, he was awake, laying on his arm and looking up at the ceiling. We were at home and I wanted to fuck.

"What you doing up, daddy?" I asked rubbing his dick. "You wanna play around a little bit?"

"I'm just thinking."

His response sounded dry and I was confused. I thought we weren't beefing anymore but I always knew when something was wrong with him. "Are you just thinking about fucking me? Or just thinking about life in general?"

He rolled his head in my direction and smiled. "You so sexy, Ginger. And beautiful. Did I tell you that lately?" he rubbed my chin and squeezed it lightly.

"You tell me all the time." I sat on his dick and looked down at him. "That's one of the reasons I'm still with you. You know how to treat a bitch."

"Now look who's calling themselves a bitch?"

I giggled. "I had to get use to the fact that's just your word, and to not take it personal." I kissed him on the chest. "As long as you not trying to play me I don't care." I looked deeply into his eyes. "But for real baby, what's on your mind?"

He sighed. "A lot, mama. Sometimes too much."

I rolled my eyes and sighed. "How come you can't ever just answer my question when I ask you one? What is on your mind, Gerron? Damn! Spit it the fuck out! I really want to know."

I exhaled. "A lot…but mainly I'm thinking about my mother, and wondering where she is and if she's okay. To be honest I don't even know if she's alive, baby. This nigga Bodie been in jail for a year. Who gonna keep her that long while he sits in there? It doesn't make sense. Something's wrong."

Gerron is so strong that sometimes I forget that his mother is being held somewhere that we don't know. I guess that's why he liked to do so many extortion jobs, to keep his mind off of her. To keep his mind off of the pain she might be in. Unlike me he was really close to his mother.

"I'm so sorry, Gerron. I can't imagine what you're going through right now. Is there anything I can do for you?"

"Outside of making sure you never get as drunk as you got the other day when we hit the dude in the eye patch, I'd say no. I don't want to see that part of you again, Ginger. It's unattractive."

151

I rolled off of him and curled up on my side. "Gerron, when are you going to ask me to be your wife?"

He laughed. Hard.

"I just told you I felt you were being unattractive and you want me to ask you to be my wife? Are you playing?" he paused. "If you want me to marry you so badly how about you ask me instead," he grinned.

"I'm not asking no nigga to marry me. If you want me in your life for eternity I want you to ask. How come I feel like you don't want to anymore? What's up with that shit?"

"I got my reasons, Ginger. That's all I can tell you."

I frowned. "So you never gonna ask me to be your wife again? That's what you saying?" I knew I sounded like a tape recorder but my feelings were fucked up.

He eased out of bed like he always did when I brought up the marriage topic. He headed toward the bathroom but I blocked him. Standing in front of him I said, "I need you to answer my fucking question. What the fuck is wrong with you? Talk to me!"

He gritted his teeth and I stared into his eyes. He wanted to hurt something I'm sure of it. "I will never ask a bitch to be my wife who cares more about being married than how I feel about my mother. Now get out of my way, Ginger, before you discover a side of me I promised never to show anybody again."

I stepped aside and he walked into the bathroom and slammed the door behind him.

We were downstairs sitting in the High Rollers lounge looking for Desmond and Ric, real estate moguls. All though they weren't here yet, it wouldn't take me long to find them. I was sure of it. They were a beautiful black couple who looked like models. They had it all, and all we wanted was to tax them a little.

Although this was business and was usually fun, my heart wasn't in it tonight. For some reason I got the impression that it's over between us, and that he didn't want to tell me. Even when we were at the house earlier today we didn't talk to one another. It's like I lost him. I guess it's true what my mother use to say to me, when we were on speaking terms anyway. That once you break a man's heart you'd have a better chance of hitting the lottery than winning it back again.

When it looked like Desmond and Ric weren't coming, I walked over to Gerron, and touched him on the arm. He was playing craps in the casino. "Make that your last one, baby. They not coming so we might as well get out of here and go home."

He nodded but didn't open his mouth. He can be so fucking petty at times. I feel bad enough for bringing up marriage when he was sharing how he felt about his mother, but it wasn't intentional. Why couldn't he just let it go and accept my apology?

As I watched the back of his head I was getting angrier. I guess this is the attitude problem I have. "Gerron, I wish you stop acting like a bitch," I blurted out.

He turned around and looked at me. Since he laughed at first I didn't hear what he said next so he said it again. "Get the fuck outta my face, bitch before I steal you in your jaw. You being reckless now."

"I'm done kissing your ass you black mothafucka." I stomped toward the exit in a hurry and with my feelings hurt. I tripped over the end of my slinky black dress and all most fell flat on my face. Luckily the chest of the guy Desmond broke my fall.

He was alone.

Desmond put one hand on my waist and said, "My bad, beautiful. I couldn't get out of your way in time." He looked over my head as if he was trying to see who was watching us. "Are you okay?"

I looked up at him. I knew he was fine but his picture didn't do him justice. I hadn't expected him to be this attractive.

"I'm okay," I smiled placing a strand of my long hair behind my ear. "Just a little clumsy but thank you."

"You're leaving so early?" he asked looking over me again. "Because I just got here and could use the good luck and company."

"I'm far from good luck."

"Let me be the judge of that."

For him to be married to Ric he was pouring it on thick. "Actually I'm kind of tired of the tables. All I want to do is go upstairs to my room."

"To sleep?"

I licked my bottom lip and looked into his eyes. "To be lonely."

He ran his fingers down the middle of my back. "Not if I can help it."

Desmond was lying in my hotel bed as I walked slowly toward him. I was wearing my pink satin nightgown with my red bra and panties underneath. Although I went upstairs to the room without Gerron, I knew he was going to be up here as soon as he could find Ric. At least I hoped so. If he didn't come soon, the way I feel I can't make any promises about what will go down between me and the man candy in the bed.

"You look good, baby," he said as his eyes looked through me. "Real sexy. So tell me, who are you with? Because anything as sexy as you can't be single."

"What I really want to know is who you are?" I said enjoying the attention he was giving me although I shouldn't be. This was business but it felt more like pleasure. "You talk real slick and real smooth. Something like a pimp."

"I'm just a man, nothing less, nothing more." He raised his arms out to his sides. "Even though it's a little too late to be asking me don't you think? After all you already invited me in. At this point I could have my way with you and nobody would ever find out."

I eased into the bed and straddled him. His dick pressed against my panties, which for the moment concealed my heated pussy. Feeling guilty I looked over at the door, and then back down at him. Where is Gerron? I don't want to be unfaithful but it's hard.

"What's up with you?" he asked with a smile on his face.

"Nothing," I shrugged.

"Why you keep looking at the door? You looked at it three times since I been up here." He removed the smile from his face. His expression changed but I don't know if I should be afraid. Not necessarily evil, but serious.

"I can't look at my door?" I said bending down to kiss him on the cheek. I wanted him to relax. "You in my room, not the other way around."

"You are about to rob me aren't you?" he asked plainly.

He said it so smoothly it was as if it didn't bother him.

"Why would I do that? I'm starting to really like you."

"You'd do it for my money." He pawed my breasts and his touch felt like positive electricity shooting throughout my body. "Why would anybody rob another person?"

I bent down and kissed him on the lips and when I raised up Gerron was standing in the room with a gun next to Ric's head. I didn't hear him come in. He really does be on some creep shit. He moves so lightly.

Ric was also prettier than her pictures. The long black hair she wore cascaded with big wavy curls down her back, and the royal blue body conscious dress that covered her frame showcased her hourglass shape.

"It took you long enough to get here," I said to Gerron. He looked angry, as if I just cheated on him or something. Maybe I did. I rolled off of Desmond's crotch and closed by robe.

"Having fun yet?" Gerron asked.

"I didn't get a chance too."

He rolled his eyes. "You pushing it with me. Real hard."

"Tell me something I don't already know," I said grabbing my glass of wine that sat on the desk across from the bed. I took a big sip and my hand shook.

"Can somebody please tell me what the fuck is going on around here?" Desmond asked us. He wasn't smiling anymore, and neither was his wife.

"You being extorted," I said. "Don't act like you don't know."

"He ain't the one with the paper," Gerron corrected me. He ran the barrel of the gun along Ric's cheekbone. "She is, and we going to take a little trip to the bank to tax her."

"So what am I supposed to do with him then?" I wanted to sound uninterested but I knew that Gerron could see right through me.

"Whatever you want," he said with a glare. "Since I know you was gonna do that shit anyway."

Gerron walked out of the door with Ric to go to the bank, leaving me alone with Desmond. He didn't know it but he gave me a pass.

He was about to get up out of the bed until I grabbed the gun inside of the pocket of my robe. I cocked it and said, "Lay back down."

"What the fuck is going on?" he responded like he still was about to get up. "This shit is serious now. Your boyfriend got Ric held at gunpoint. I don't understand."

"How could you be confused? You even asked me if I was going to rob you a few minutes ago. What's changed now? That your precious wife is involved? This is the major league, baby. I'm not interested in the money you got in the wallet in your pants. We about that big paper you holding in the bank."

"When I asked if you were about to rob me I didn't know that you realized that...that ..."

"That your woman had the money and not you?" I laughed finishing his sentence. "My beau does his homework. Trust me. Besides, if he took you to the bank and you came up broke, he would've killed you. Technically your wife is saving your life, and you should be grateful." I walked over to the bed with the gun still aimed. "Now lay the fuck down."

He lied down and I straddled him again. With the gun pointed at his head, while I sat on top of him, I removed my robe so that it fell over my shoulders. I could feel his dick stiffen in his boxers and I smiled. He was the right size and I knew we would have a lot of fun together.

"What are you about to do?" he asked in a low voice. "Rape me?"

"Whatever you want to tell your wife, for the reason you cheated, works for me."

"What about your man?"

I looked at the door again and then down at him. "You heard him. He doesn't care about me so why should I care about him. I'm mad, and when I'm mad I get even."

"By having sex with another man? You remind me of my wife."

I shrugged.

I released his dick from his boxers and pushed my black panties to the side. I grabbed a condom from my robe, and slid it on with one hand. He tried to act irritated, but anticipation danced behind his eyes. I could tell he wanted this. He wanted me.

When his dick was dressed and ready to go, I slid on top of him. I didn't know when it was going to stop. It felt as if he was filling me up for days. When he was fully inside of me, he grabbed my waist and fucked me hard. I licked my lips because fucking him felt better than I imagined. When he got too rough, and pumped into me so hard I fell to the side, I placed the gun to his forehead. He wasn't in control of this shit, I was.

Desmond pumped in and out of me, forcing shivers throughout my entire body.

I was in ecstasy.

CHAPTER 22

GERRON

Ric was driving the car on the way back to the hotel while I laid back in the passenger seat. Although she had a small waist, my gun stayed trained on it in case she got out of hand. I was right about who held the reigns to the bank account. This fine bitch was able to withdraw fifty thousand dollars like it wasn't shit. But it didn't feel good, not the way it use to when we scored.

I knew what felt different; I just didn't want to say it out loud. I couldn't get the look in Ginger's eyes out of my mind. When I walked into the room and saw the expression on her face, as she sat on top of old boy, it made my stomach churn and I wanted to hurt her and him. That shit wasn't business. It was pleasure. If I didn't know how much she had my head wrapped up, I knew after that.

"What you thinking about over there?" Ric asked me placing a long strand of hair behind her ear.

My baby do that shit too. At that time I started realizing that they had a lot in common. They both were powerful. I could tell by looking in Ric's eyes what type of shawty she was. But she didn't know her strength.

Now I want to know about Ric and Desmond's relationship, which I normally don't do.

"Why did you withdraw the money to save him, when you saw what he was doing with my bitch?"

She smiled and continued to pilot the car. "It's obvious that there is a lot about life you don't know. That you don't understand, but I'm not surprised. Considering your occupation."

"Help me understand then."

She giggled a little and then dipped in front of a slow Suburban that was driving in front of us. "Desmond is not the worthless piece of shit that he appears to be," she smiled. "He's so much more."

I wasn't buying it. "You have to tell me more than that if you want me to believe you because I still don't get it. You and I both know what was going to go on in that room if we didn't show up when we did."

She seemed sad. "I had a year long affair behind Desmond's back, when we first got married." She looked at me and then back at the road. "Him walking in on me giving another man oral sex wasn't the worst part, it was the look in his eyes when he caught us in our bed. You a man so I know you can vouch for this. Women have always accepted men's infidelities, but men find it so hard to forgive ours." A tear fell down her face and she let it roll. "Even if he didn't dump me I knew it was over. So when he closed the door I finished his friend off."

"Whoa," I said shaking my head. "So you couldn't get a hotel? You had to do it in ya'll bed? Bitches kill me."

"You don't know shit about me. While you over there passing judgment you should know that people make mistakes."

"It's still some foul shit."

"So you never slept with someone who was taken? Or fucked her in her boyfriend's house?" she raised her eyebrows as if she knew my truth. "Ever?"

I thought about Ginger, and how I fucked her on the couch Milli bought for her when we first got together. Shawty caught me and all I could do was shake my head and smile.

"I thought so," she responded. "I was wrong for what I did, don't get me wrong, but I made a mistake. I just wanted something more and I never knew what until that moment. It wasn't anything more than sex really. Desmond was just a great man who felt inadequate because he couldn't provide the lifestyle I was accustomed to. It affected our relationship so I cheated with a close friend."

"I feel you," I lied. I had my shit with me but friends were off limits.

"I'm just a woman who made a mistake." She pulled over to the side of the road.

"What the fuck is you doing?" I asked stabbing her waist with the barrel. "Keep driving. We almost at the hotel."

"Be easy," she said parking the car. "I just want to talk to you for five seconds, Gerron."

"How did you know my name?"

"I have my ways."

"How did you know my fucking name?"

"Your girl said it under her breath when you walked in on her."

This shit was getting out of hand. "If you don't pull this car back onto the road I'm gonna blow a hole in your head," I yelled. "Don't think just because you a bitch that I won't do it."

No matter how loud I yelled she wasn't listening. "Calm down, all I want to do is help you with a little piece of revenge."

"What the fuck does that mean?"

She moved her hands toward my crotch and I backed up against the door. Even though I had the gun on her it was like I was handing her flowers. She didn't care and I felt like she had the power. So I sat the barrel on the bridge of her nose.

"I'm not fuckin' with you. Put this car back on the road."

"You're not going to shoot me."

"You don't know shit about me or what I will do." I cocked the gun. "Now drive."

She smiled. Not like she was testing my limits, but almost like she knew something I didn't. "You won't murder me because you're not a killer unless somebody gives you a firm reason. All I want to do is make you smile. Where is the harm in that?"

And why would you want to make me smile? I just got you for fifty stacks."

"I'm a very wealthy woman, Gerron. Which I don't have to tell you because like you said, you taxed me already. But what you probably don't know is that I'm bored. My husband doesn't touch me anymore, and yet I saw the look in his eyes as your girlfriend sat on top of him. I want someone to look at me like that, even if I have to pay for it. I've been praying for a release and to feel like a woman again." She looked around and there were no cars near us. "I think my prayers have been answered on the side of a dirt road in Nevada. You took my money and you can have it," she looked in the back seat. "I won't fight you for it. All I want is for you to take me too. You do this and I'll be forever indebted to you."

I lowered the gun and she lowered her head, giving me the best blowjob of my life.

CHAPTER 23

GINGER

I'm lying in our bed looking at Gerron. His back is faced my direction. We're at home. Everything about this last hit felt different. Normally after a hit Gerron would be back within three hours with the money, but this time he didn't come back until four o'clock in the morning. Where was he? With her?

"Gerron," I said softly placing my cold hand on his shoulder. "You up?"

He moaned. "Naw."

If he wasn't up how could he answer? I stared at him, not saying another word because I didn't want to fight again. He must've felt me holding back my anger because he turned around and looked at me.

"I cheated on you last night," we both said at the same time.

My eyes widened. I couldn't believe that he was being honest with me; at the same time I was being honest with him. And then it hit me. The pain in my chest. He fucked another woman. Did he want to be with her now?

"Who did you sleep with?" I asked.

His voice was deep due to just waking up. He cleared his throat and said, "Who you think?"

I closed my eyes and tears fell down my cheek. I wiped them away and sighed. "Ric? His wife?"

"Yeah."

"I guess I shouldn't be upset or hurt huh? I'm no better than you."

"No, you not."

"Then why do I feel like my heart is broken?"

He sighed. "We fucked outside of our relationship, Ginger. I didn't want it to happen but it did. Maybe we needed to get it out of our system to realize we want to be together. I don't know." He shrugged. "If we can move past this maybe we can work."

"Say I believe that, are you gonna be mad at me forever? Are you gonna always hold over my head the fact that I brought up Milli's name when I had no idea that you were about to ask me to be your wife? Because that's where our real problem started, Gerron. We been good up to this point."

"We haven't been good in months. That's the thing you don't realize. I always felt that you was holding the fact that I wasn't him over my head. It just came out on the day I was about to give my life to you that's all. I'm a man, Ginger. And I felt played."

"But I love you," I said touching his face. "I wish I could take what I did back, but I can't."

"You love me but you fucked another nigga."

167

I frowned. "And you fucked another bitch!" I reminded him.

He looked at me, and his mouth moved like he was going to ask me something but he didn't know how. I been with him long enough to know the question though, even though he didn't say the words.

"No," I said softly. "Not even close."

"No what?"

"No he wasn't better than you."

"How you know I was going to ask you that?" he grinned.

"Because we kindred spirits, Gerron. And I'm not talking about some fluffy shit people say when they feeling some kind of way. I believe you been the real one all along, and I didn't realize it until we fought at the restaurant and I thought I lost you. I never loved Milli. I loved what I thought he could do for me."

"If we be together I can't feel like I'm gonna always be compared to him when you get mad, Ginger. I don't like the feeling. It makes me want to snap."

"And you will never be compared to him ever again."

"What about with the other man?"

"That shit is never happening again. I felt so bad about what I did that I almost killed him because I didn't want you finding out when you came back with Ric. It was an epic fail giving that dude some pussy. You got my heart, Gerron, and I am totally over Milli. All I want to do is be your wife but I know I have to move like one first."

He rubbed my arm. "We got one more job and then we done, Ginger. I don't want this life for us no more. We got enough paper so that even if this nigga Bodie gets out and takes the one hundred grand we'll still be good."

I finished eating my steak and looked over at Gerron. We were in the first restaurant we came to when we stepped into Nevada. I always looked at the diner as the place he took me on our first date. Because the moment we got off the plane we grabbed a bite to eat here, and we had been together ever since.

He was smiling more since we had our talk the other day and I was confident that things were going to work out between us. If we never fought again in our lifetime it would be too soon for me. I realized I wanted him and that I was going to have to take a backseat on some things...especially my attitude. Gerron was right. He was my man and although I felt like I had to play both roles in my relationship with Milli, by being a man and a woman, I don't have to do that with him. I was going to follow his lead because with Gerron I knew there was no losing.

"What you smiling for?" I asked chewing my meat.

"Us, because we finally done with this hood life."

I look down at the scraps of food on my plate. "But are you gonna be okay with that, Gerron?"

"What you mean?"

"You love this life, baby. It's adventure for you and gets your blood rolling. If you get out the game what else are you going to do with your time? Sticking niggas up is all you know."

"You right and if I get the urge I'll do it about once a year." He chuckled. "But at the end of the day we have more money than we ever dreamed of, Ginger. We gonna get out, find us a new place in Mexico somewhere and get our family back. That's the only thing on my mind right now. Not banking niggas."

My heart thumped just thinking about the plan. I imagined shopping for my daughter. I imagined doing her hair. I imagined holding her, and telling her that everything in her life was going to be okay. I imagined peace with Gerron and our family.

"You think we really gonna be able to get your mother and my daughter back?"

"I'm positive. Even if I have to die doing it. We will see their smiling faces again, baby. You gotta trust me."

I drank my wine and looked down at my hands. I'm not a mushy girl, but I had to admit, I was excited about the idea of being serious with him. When I looked up, Gerron was standing up with a man dressed in a dark blue suit. How did he do that? We could be home and I would be in a room alone. I would turn my head and when I'd looked back he would be there. He moved light. If he wasn't a stick up nigga I could easily see him being a ballerina, but he hated when I played like that.

A few people that were eating were now standing around him. Like everybody knew what was going on but me. "Ginger, I know we been through a lot," he said with serious eyes. "And I know this place is cheesy, but it represents the start of our lives together. So I'm asking you will you marry me but I'm not waiting for us to fight again. I'm not waiting for another chance of doubt to fill our relationship. If you want to be my wife I want to do it right here and right now. So what do you want to do? Will you do me the honor of being Mrs. Gerron Mantis?"

I covered my mouth, leaped up and hugged him. I was probably squeezing him too hard but I wanted him to know how much I cared. To feel my heartbeat against his chest. I had been waiting to be a wife all of my life and it was finally going to happen. I wasn't worried about marrying him right here because I knew I would have a more official ceremony later.

"Baby, is this a game?"

"I'm not playing games with you no more. I knew you were the one for me the moment you first moved 'round Kentland. It was confirmed for me the first day I first touched your body. I just needed you to know too."

He reached into his pocket and grabbed a blue velvet box. He popped it open and another beautiful diamond ring was staring at me. "I didn't want you to have the same ring so I traded it up for something better. So are you gonna marry me?"

"You know I want to be your wife, Gerron. I don't want anything else in my life more."

He smiled and slid the ring on my finger. And right there, in a small restaurant we were married by a Vegas minister who he paid $75.00. It wasn't elaborate or anything I would write home about. Me and Gerron didn't say anything profound, or anything I would tell our future children we would have together. It was what we didn't say, and the way we looked into each other's eyes that I will remember.

When we were married he put his arm around my shoulder. "Now that you my wife, let me hit that pussy harder since it got my name on it."

My stomach fluttered and we were about to walk out of the restaurant as husband and wife until his new cell phone rang. With a smile on his face he said, "hello."

I grinned as I looked up at him. I was his wife! But then his facial expression changed. He didn't look like the man who was happy he was just married to the love of his life. His mood went from pleasure to anger.

"What's wrong, baby?" I asked him in a soft voice.

He put his finger up at me and said to the caller, "Yeah, I want to speak to her." He looked at me but I couldn't decipher what was going on. "Hey, ma," he said looking into my eyes, "don't worry about anything, I'm coming for you."

CHAPTER 24

GINGER

I'm standing in the hotel elevator with Gerron. Alone. We are about to hunt for our last and final mark at another hotel all because Bodie got extra greedy. He just got out of jail and instead of taking the initial ransom, he wanted half a million dollars. Somebody told him we were sitting on money, and I had a feeling the Indian dude Hassan did his homework and turned the streets on us. As much as I wanted my husband reunited with his moms, I had a sinking feeling in the pit of my stomach that if we robbed one more person it wouldn't end good.

As the elevator crept down I approached him. "Let's not do this, baby."

He looked over my head, and at the monitor indicating which floor the elevator was on. "What you talking about?"

"I don't have a good feeling about this." He looked down at me. "I had a dream last night and in it we died. Please listen to me. Let's just meet up with Bodie, give him the money we got and hope for the best."

"You heard him, Ginger. The nigga wants a half of mill. We only got four hundred and fifty, which means we short. I'm not taking no chance with this dude. I want my moms safe."

"G, Bodie's a dopehead who will take what he can get. Trust me. If we show up with—"

"You not listening," he yelled interrupting me. He screamed so hard one of my curls blew out of my face. "The nigga got my moms and I'm not gonna chance it thinking he playing games. I rather hit somebody for fifty grand and you need to understand that—"

I pushed the emergency stop button on the elevator and interrupted his statement. The elevator jolted and knocked us around a little. The loud alarm ringing was annoying but I was determined to remain focused and get my point across. I'd rather die in this elevator, with my husband, then outside on the streets without saying my piece.

"What the fuck you doing?" He asked holding the gold rail behind him.

I placed both of my hands on the sides of his face and looked into his eyes. I was calm but I was firm. "If...we...do...this...job...we...will...die." When I saw I held his attention I released his face. "I don't want to lose you, Gerron." I laid my face against his hard chest. "I just found you. We just found each other. Please, I'm begging you."

He looked down at me, and I felt he finally understood what was at stake. Our lives.

"You right, Ginger. If we do this there's a possibility that we may die. My only question to you is are you willing to die with me?"

I looked up into his eyes and smiled. "Yes." I exhaled. "Even if it means going to hell."

This couple we decided on wasn't our usual type. Josep was a drug dealer and Kim, his bitch, was a loud-mouthed physician's assistant. It was a classic case of bad boy meets good girl and turns her into a rotten whore. Or for all we knew, it was the other way around.

Josep looked like he had every chain he owned around his neck. His girlfriend wore a gold wig so bad the net under it was showing. They both were a mess but Gerron assured me that he peeped dude going back and forth to his room to get some cash for the tables. I tried not to think about the fact that Gerron was only concerned with his mother, and might be moving by his feelings instead of his head. A dangerous way to operate. I really wanted to trust him.

"So what ya'll do for a living?" Kim asked me as she sat on the sofa in our suite sipping vodka.

Although me, Josep and Kim were on the sofa, Gerron was pacing around behind us like a lunatic. He was making everybody uncomfortable including me, his partner.

"We don't like to talk about ourselves," I responded.

"You know what, none of this shit matters," Gerron responded whipping his weapon out of his pocket. He wasn't smooth with it at all. "You know what time it is, baby boy."

I pulled my gun out on Kim.

"You gotta be fucking kidding me," Josep whined. "Please God, tell me this ain't no set up." He placed his hands over his face. "Please tell me this is a joke and the four of us really about to fuck like ya'll said we was."

"This ain't about God, my nigga, and it's definitely not no joke. This here is about them stacks you sitting on in your room. You 'bout to take me to them or I'ma murk this ugly bitch on your arm."

"Ugly?" she responded with her jaw hung. "Who the fuck you talking to?"

"You heard him, whore," I replied.

"I don't got no money," Josep replied. "So if ya'll doing this then it's all for nothing."

"For both of your sakes I hope it ain't true, man," Gerron said. "At this point I ain't got nothing to lose."

"What if I don't give you shit?"

Gerron came down on his head with the gun, splitting his ear open. When he was done he placed the barrel on his upper lip. "You want me to use the other end next and blow your face off?"

"Wait a minute, so are ya'll saying we not gonna fuck for real?" Kim asked as if she wasn't watching what was going on all this time. The last thing folks were thinking about was sex.

"That question been answered already," I said with an attitude.

"And I wouldn't fuck you with this nigga's dick," Gerron said.

"Hold up, my man, ain't no need in disrespecting my baby's mother."

"You got a kid?" Gerron asked with raised eyebrows.

I could tell by the look on Gerron's face that he didn't like our plan anymore. He was probably feeling bad because they were parents. But I don't know what he expected. We robbed plenty of people and chances are fifty percent of them had kids too. At the end of the day we already made our decision and now it was time to push off.

"She's pregnant with my baby right now," Josep said still holding his bloody ear. "So you can't touch her or you'll kill my seed."

"And you trying to fuck somebody with that pregnant ass pussy? I said squinting my nose up.

"Pregnant girls need love too."

"Listen, as long as you be easy I don't see no reason to split your girl or your baby open with no bullet," Gerron said. "But if you fuck with me and not give me every dime you got in this hotel there's gonna be problems you gonna be left to deal with at the funeral. Hear me?"

Josep exhaled. I could tell he was angry and I wasn't sure how things were going to work out. For starters Gerron had to get Josep to his room without other people watching them. But since blood was pouring out of his ear I knew being discreet was next to difficult.

"I'm not gonna give you no trouble, just tell your bitch not to touch my girl. That's all I'm saying. I don't want my baby hurt."

After Gerron assisted Josep with cleaning the blood off of his face in the bathroom, they left the room leaving me and Kim alone. I got a bad feeling about this shit.

"You know this not gonna end good right?" Kim said to me. "I'm just saying."

My heart pounded. "Why you say that?"

"Because I had a dream this would happen and it didn't end good."

"For who?" I asked.

"For us. All of us."

CHAPTER 25

GINGER

I was sitting across from her— judging her. It was pretty fucked up now that I think about it. Here I was a new wife, who didn't have her own child because she was taken from her by the office of child support. Yet I had all intentions of murdering this so-called mother to be if she made a move.

"You not pregnant," I told her as I made sure my gun remained trained on her.

She smirked. In a way that told me that game recognized game. She leaned back into the sofa, grabbed a pack of cigarettes from the table and lit one. She took her time allowing the smoke to fill her lungs before pressing fluffy clouds above her head. "How you know?"

"I can tell by how you move."

She laughed. "You're so right. There is no way in the world I would let that nigga nut me up and get me pregnant. Whether you believe me or not, I am going to school to be a doctor, and I can't have him getting in my way."

"Good for you," I shrugged.

"I do have a question for you."

"And what's that?"

"If you're so smart why are you doing this shit?"

"By this shit do you mean making money?"

"I mean playing with your life." She crossed her legs. "Josep is a very important man, sweetheart." She took a few more pulls. "So am I and the people we know. None of us are going to take this shit lightly."

"I'm not worried about no Josep or you. By the time he gets ready to do anything we'll be clear across the country."

She seemed angry. "You do this shit all the time don't you? Taking other people's hard earned money. That's your idea of a career choice?"

I didn't respond.

"But you not a killer," she continued. "I can see straight through your brown skin and into your green interior."

"Bitch, you have no idea what I am."

"I know a killer when I see one, and you, boo boo are not. Sure you may have busted your gun a few times, and you might have even met your target by accident. But as far as the heart goes, you not a killer and it ain't in you."

This bitch was making me mad. How the fuck did she think she know so much about me? And more importantly, why was she so right?

"If you want to test my heart all you have to do is make a move. I will blow your head back if I have to just to prove my point. Trust me."

She stood up and a sly grin rested upon her face. She switched toward me. "No you won't."

I leaped up too. "Don't fuck with me," I told her. "I will unload this bitch into your body if you take another step. I'm warning you."

She stopped moving. And as if she was about to blow me a kiss she puckered her lips and said, "Then…shoot…me…bitch."

With that she leapt on top of me and the gun flew out of my hand. She gripped my hair and I pressed my thumbs into her eye sockets. But this bitch had the strength reserved for niggas lifting weights behind bars. She was able to pull both of my hands from her face, and then she slammed me in the center of the nose with a closed fist. I immediately swallowed my own blood and tried to regain control of the situation. Eventually I was able to get a hold of her hair but the wig came off. And then she did it. Grabbed a hold of my gun.

I quickly climbed on her back like a coat before she could turn around and shoot me. We wrestled with the gun and her hand was on the trigger. I was about to lose my life. This was the day I was going to die I could feel it.

She was able to strong-arm me off of her and before I knew it the gun was pressed against my temple. She cocked it. With a devilish smile and her salty sweat dripping in my mouth she said, "You dreamed about me too didn't you?"

Silence.

"You should've heeded the warning in your nightmares," she continued.

With the gun pointed at my head, I closed my eyes, said a silent prayer for Gerron and Denise and she pulled the trigger. But I wasn't dead. Where was the boom or the pain associated with being shot? The gun jammed and I survived.

I took this as my reason to fight and with the little strength I had left I hit her so hard in the face, her cheek shifted and I heard the snap of her jaw. The gun flew out of her hand and while she tended to her loose mouth, I went for my weapon.

Finally on my feet I looked down at her.

"Don't move, Kim," I said breathing heavily.

I wanted to say something witty. Something that she would remember on her trip to hell. But for the life of me I couldn't think of anything.

So I saved myself the trouble and just pulled the trigger.

When Gerron came back with Josep holding the briefcase filled with money, I was pacing the floor like a maniac. He knew immediately that something was wrong the moment he saw my face. I could see it in his eyes.

"Where's my baby's mother?" Josep asked looking behind me at the closed bedroom door. "You said if I gave you the paper you would leave her alone. So where is she?"

I didn't respond.

"You didn't baby," Gerron whispered.

"I didn't have a choice."

Without wasting time Gerron walked up to Josep. "Hey, man, I'm sorry about that shit"— He put the trigger to Josep's head and pulled— "but your girl is gone and so are you."

Josep's brains splattered over the door and the brown ice bucket on the table. For a second we both just looked at him.

Gerron tucked his gun in his waist and asked, "Baby, are you okay? I tried to get back as quick as I could."

I couldn't talk. I knew something bad was going to happen and it was.

Gerron held me in his arms and rocked me. "I'm so sorry, baby. You told me that you didn't want to come." He gripped me tighter. "I should have listened."

I wiped my tears. "What we gonna do now?"

BAM! BAM! BAM!

There was a heavy knock on the door. It sounded like the cops. I was worried that it was until I heard a frantic female's voice. "Housekeeping, I heard a gunshot in there! Is everyone okay?"

Gerron pressed his finger against his lips, looked at me and said, "Shhhhhhh."

"Housekeeping, is everyone okay?" the maid repeated louder.

Sweat trickled down my face. We needed to get the fuck out of here. There were two dead bodies in the hotel room and we were covered in blood and gunpowder residue. Our fate depended on the maid minding her own fucking business. We were definitely federally fucked if she used her key and came into the room.

As we waited on the maid's reaction Gerron looked down at me. He was as still as a statue. We both were.

"I'm going to get the police," the maid said.

Fuck!

CHAPTER 26

GERRON

Ginger and I were standing in front of each other. My hands were on both sides of her face, and nothing but our breath could be heard in the room. I wanted her to look into my eyes and know that as my wife, I would do all I could to protect her...from here until eternity.

"We gonna be okay," I finally said. "No matter what happens."

"I know." She bit down on her bottom lip. "I'm with you and that's all that ever mattered."

"I'm sorry about this shit, babes."

"Sorry not gonna get us out of here. Fighting for our lives will."

Little by little I could finally hear the police sirens in the background. They had been there all along but we finally heard them. I released her face and walked over to the window. There was a sea of cop cars flashing their blue, white and red lights and they were all looking for us. There was nowhere to run. I didn't have a plan.

In survival mode I rushed into the bathroom and grabbed the two duffle bags filled with money. I took the money out of the briefcase that I got from Josep and stuffed it inside one of the duffels. I put one over my shoulder and handed Ginger the other. I had an extra gun so I gave Ginger two and I kept one.

"If we get separated, you take that bag and leave the country like we talked about. Okay?"

She frowned. "I'm never leaving your side, Gerron. Why can't you understand that?"

"I hear you but—"

"I'm not fucking leaving you," she screamed. "So either we gonna stay here and wait for the cops to get locked up, or we gonna go out blazing. Whatever we do it's gonna be together because without you I have nothing to lose. Even my daughter is better off without me as far as I'm concerned."

She's stubborn but it's one of the things I liked about her. With the money, and our weapons, I grabbed my wife's hand. We moved slowly to the door and I looked out of the peephole. I didn't see anybody so I opened the door—carefully.

When I saw an old man standing in front of his door I snatched Ginger out of the room, walked in his direction, aimed at him and said, "Stay right there, old man. I don't want to kill you but I will if I have to."

He raised both of his hands in the air and Ginger got his key and opened his door. We walked inside of his room and I was thrown off by the collection of wigs that were lined up on the dresser. There was a red one, a brown one, a blonde one, a black one and I looked over at the frightened man who was trembling.

"You some freaky ass cross dresser?" I asked him. Ginger and I had the guns on him.

"I wish my life was that interesting." He swallowed. "They belong to my wife. She's downstairs playing BINGO."

I looked over at Ginger and said, "I got an idea."

I never wore a dress in my life and if I make it out of this alive I will never do it again. I'm wearing this long blue sheet like dress that Ginger called a Muumuu along with a short black wig. I fucked with the outfit for now because I was able to wear my real clothes under it since it was baggy. Ginger was wearing a yellow Muumuu with a red wig and she didn't look anywhere as bad as me. The only other thing we wore were the duffle bags around our shoulders stacked with cash. It was our best accessory.

"Alright, Old Man, I know you gonna tell the cops you saw us." I reached into the bag and handed him a stack of cash. "But I'm hoping this will buy your wife some new wigs, and a lie in our favor. All I'm asking is that you tell the police we wearing something else if you tell them anything at all. What do you say?"

He took the stack and smiled and I accepted that as a yes.

"When we walk out of this door move slow and old," I told my wife.

"Gerron, I don't feel like doing all of that."

"Just do it. Dressed like this we have to play the part."

We dipped out of the room. The room where the bodies are was all the way down the other end of the hall. When we opened the door we didn't see any cops, which was a good look. But where were they? At this point I'd think the floor would be flooded with police.

I pulled Ginger out of the room and we moved slowly toward the exit closest to the Old Man's room. When all of a sudden a cop yelled, "Don't move!"

Ginger turned around. I remained with my back faced them because I made an ugly ass woman and I didn't want them knowing who I really was.

"Yes, sir," she said with a quivering voice.

"You two need to get off of this floor right now. We have some crazed killers on the loose and I don't want you getting hurt. They're in this room right here, and things are about to get dangerous."

"Yes, sir," Ginger responded in a weak voice. "We'll be leaving right now."

I couldn't believe my luck. With the cops approval we slowly walked out of the door and then darted down the stairwell.

"Good looking out on the moving slow thing, baby," Ginger said. "I guess they really believed we were old women."

"Maybe one day you'll learn to trust me because I got us, Ginger." We continued to run down the steps.

When we made it to the lowest floor the door opened. I pushed Ginger up against the wall and said, "Shhhh."

I aimed my gun at the door to see who was coming inside. A gray bin rolled in first followed by a mailman. His eyes opened wide when he saw us. "I'm sorry ma'am, I was..."

He stopped talking and his eyes widened. He wagged his finger from left to right and said, "Wait a minute! You're the two! You're the two they're looking for. They flashed your pictures on the news, from a surveillance camera in the hotel. Why are you dressed like...women?"

Before I could respond he ran out of the door but I was right behind him. He was screaming to the top of his lungs and moving toward a pile of police cars in front of the hotel. At the moment none of them were faced in our direction, which was on the side of the hotel. They were getting out of the car and moving toward the front.

"It's them! It's them," he screamed.

I was able to get to him before the police heard him. I jumped on his back and his face slammed into the concrete. He was knocked out cold. I pulled the black wig off of my head and then the dress. I took the mailman shirt he was wearing off and grabbed the keys from his belt chain.

I turned around and looked at Ginger. She looked stuck. "Come on, baby." I stood up. "We gotta go."

She hesitated at first but then she followed me to the mailman's car. I jumped into the driver's seat, which was on the right side, and we pulled off. I adjusted the rearview mirror and could still see that the police had their backs facing our direction as we drove away. We were safe.

Ginger didn't feel calm though. She kept rubbing her legs and turning around to look behind us.

"It's gonna be okay, baby. Relax."

"They know it's us. You heard them, Gerron. What the fuck are we going to do?"

"Maybe it's not as bad as he said it was. Maybe the picture was grainy."

She shook her head and turned on the radio. The first few stations were talking regular shit until she heard a newscaster's calm voice.

"Police are looking for an African-American man and woman who murdered Josep Walker the son of mayor Rodney Dense of Nevada, and his girlfriend Kim Waltz who was going to school to become a doctor. Gerron and Ginger Mantis are armed and considered extremely dangerous. If you see them do not attempt to apprehend them yourselves. Call authorities."

Ginger and I both looked at each other. "Josep was the mayor's son?" I said.

Her head dropped and she started to cry.

We were in over our heads now.

Way over.

CHAPTER 27

GINGER

I was standing outside with my feet embedded into the sand. I'm in the desert, wearing a Muumuu and watching Gerron park the mail truck next to some dry bushes. When I looked to my right, and then my left, there was nothing but miles and miles of yellow sand. After he parked the mail truck he walked over to me and touched my back softly. Together we approached the silver Civic with a scared family inside. They were a beautiful black family complete with a father, mother and daughter.

Gerron opened the passenger door and said, "Get out."

The woman didn't move. "Why are you doing this?" she asked him. "All we did was give you a hand when you said your mail truck was broken down. We don't deserve to be treated like this."

"Well I'm not a mailman and that's not my truck. Now get the fuck out of the car right now before I hurt you."

"Watch your language in front of my child," the father said from behind the driver's seat. It didn't matter if they stayed inside because I had the keys to the car in my hand. They couldn't go anywhere. "I won't tolerate you disrespecting my family."

"And I won't tolerate you disrespecting my life," Gerron said. "Get out of the car before I go off. Now!"

As they slowly stepped out of the car I whispered to Gerron. "He's right you know. It was wrong to curse in front of the little girl."

Normally Gerron wasn't like this. He was respectful to old people and children.

"Ginger, we are on the run for our lives," he said softly. "And you coming at me about cursing in front of some kid? Are you serious?"

I rolled my eyes and crossed my arms over my chest. I didn't feel like arguing with him right now. We had to stick together.

When the family got out of the car Gerron walked up to them. Although he didn't have the gun out, I knew he had it available and wouldn't hesitate to use it if need be. My only hope was that they didn't give him a reason to.

"As you know already we got your cell phones," he patted his jeans pocket, "and your car."

"But how are we gonna get out of here?" The wife asked looking around the desert. "We'll die if you leave us here."

"Mommy, I'm scared," the little girl whined. She looked like she was about seven.

"You'll be okay, baby," the mother responded pulling her closer to her body. "This will be all over soon."

"Let me finish." Gerron exhaled. I could tell he was becoming unraveled by all of this. Maybe the pressure of trying to take care of me, his precious new wife, was getting to him. "Like I was saying we have your car keys and your cell phones. In an hour you're going to walk about a mile down"— he pointed over their heads— "You'll find a bush with a red wig hanging from it. Walk toward it and the keys to the mail truck and the cell phone will be there. Grab the keys, walk back to the truck and drive away."

"How do I know you aren't lying?" the father asked Gerron. "You're nothing more than a common criminal."

Gerron's eyebrows pulled together. "You don't have a choice, mothafucka. I'm the one who's holding all the cards not your bitch ass. You can either believe me or stand here and die."

The father's head lowered and his wife and daughter walked toward him. For some reason I felt bad for the father. To be put in a position where you can't take care of your family must be hard. But I had to support my man and for the moment that is what I intended on doing.

Gerron walked toward the Civic. We were both about to get inside until he said, "I'm sorry about the foul language in front of your daughter. I mean...I know

I'm a thug, but I got a family too." He looked over at me. "And all I want to do is protect me and mine."

The father nodded. We hopped in the car and sped off.

In that moment I fell deeper in love with Gerron. I felt like with him there was a possibility that he could save me, and there would be a happily ever after for us. And that's why I was certain that the feeling wouldn't last.

We were driving to Arizona and as I sat in the passenger seat, I realized I was stuck— mentally and physically. Outside of the fact that we murdered the mayor's son, abandoned a family in the desert and was going to pay a ransom to get his mother, I couldn't figure out what else was wrong with me.

"That little girl reminded you of Denise didn't she?" Gerron asked me.

I exhaled. It wasn't until he asked me that question that I realized why I felt so weak. "I want to be back with my daughter, Gerron. Badly."

"I didn't want to tell you this but I made some calls. I know some folks who know Milli's wife."

Even though I was married now, when I heard Tracey being referred to as Milli's wife my stomach sank. I guess it was residue of a past relationship and broken heart. It will pass along with the feelings I had for Milli.

"So? What's your point?" I asked him.

"Well I found out they went out of town recently, Milli and Tracey. And they left Denise with Stevie. That so-called friend of yours who I had to pull you from when she tried to kill you in the front of her house. "

I looked at him. "Are you saying that Milli was bold enough to leave my daughter with one of the women he was sleeping with behind my back? And Tracey's back too? The one who is the mother to all of his kids?"

"Yes."

My fist clenched and my face tightened. "How do I know they won't hurt my baby? I'm telling you, Gerron, I'm not sure if Milli really loves his daughter or not. I feel like he would do anything he could to hurt me for leaving him and running off with you."

"I hope the nigga not that cruddy. But I can tell you this, I know some dudes who for a little money have promised that they will go up in that house, put everybody to sleep and take your daughter out of there. I'm already on it. All we gotta do is hook up with Bodie in Arizona, get my mother back and then I'll put my dudes on Denise."

"You think it will work?"

"If you believe it will."

I didn't say anything else. I just wanted to be alone in my thoughts.

After driving for twelve hours throughout the night, it was morning again. We were driving to a deserted mall in Arizona. It was the place Bodie was supposed to meet us. My right leg wouldn't stop moving and when I looked over at Gerron his face was as stiff as stone.

As we drove up a hill I couldn't believe my eyes. There was a blue Suburban parked on the side of the road. I almost choked on my air when I saw who was sitting in the driver's seat and passenger side of the truck.

"Gerron, are you seeing what I'm seeing?"

He pulled over and parked. We were at least one hundred feet away from the truck. "Yeah, baby. I do."

"Can you say it out loud, because I need to make sure I'm not tripping?"

"I see my mother, and your daughter who is sitting in the passenger seat."

I put my hands over my mouth. "And they're smiling." My daughter wasn't even supposed to be here. I looked over at him. "Did you plan this, baby? As a surprise?"

"Naw, babes, this ain't me. I don't know what your kid doing here."

When two men walked from behind the truck, and to the front of it, I realized the party was over. It was Bodie and my ex-boyfriend Milli.

Together.

When did they hook up?

CHAPTER 28

BODIE
HOW BODIE AND MILLI CAME TO BE

Bodie sat his naked ass on the brown torn sofa in his house. His limp dick rested against the inside of his thigh, yet he was holding a conversation as if he were wearing a full business suit.

"Johnson, don't fuck around with me, are you sure about this shit?"

Johnson, who was sitting on the green recliner across from him, tried to keep his stare on his eyes and not his dick. Although Bodie just got home, and was on probation, he was already looking to score some dope and money. Trouble followed his ass everywhere he went.

"Man, I swear this lead is solid. This dope house is run by two bitches— Sharon and Tina. To throw people off they both hold full time jobs at the telephone company. So what do they do Monday through Friday?"

"What?"

"At 'bout twelve o'clock pm they leave to go to work and leave their fifteen year old boy cousin, Martin,

to look over the dope until they come home about nine
o'clock at night. Anyway I know this girl who fucks with
their cousin name Erica. And Martin be letting this
chick over the house when Sharon and Tina not home.
On the day we give her, Erica is going to drug Martin
and leave the door unlocked so we can get in. That way
you can run up in that bitch and take all the work."

Bodie knew it was too good to be true but he was
greedy. He had people looking for him, like Milli and a
few other dudes, but he couldn't resist the desire to get
paid and high. He just had to be in shit.

"But what do you want out of it?" Bodie asked
him.

"Just fifteen percent of whatever you make when
you sell it."

Bodie smiled slyly. Not only was he not going to
give him shit, he couldn't wait to tell him to his face.
Besides, he was doing all of the hard work. Why should
Johnson profit? "If this works out the way I want you'll
get twenty percent."

Johnson smiled. "You got a deal."

On the day he was hitting the dope house, Bodie
was so greedy that instead of soliciting help he decided
to go by himself. So he caught the bus to the apartment

complex, rushed toward the building and crawled up the stairs like a prowler.

When he made it to the door, he turned the knob, pushed it open and removed the weapon from his waist. The moment he walked inside he was staring at Milli. Behind him were four hard-hitting niggas, including Milli's uncle Kettle. Milli was dressed in all black with a gold diamond chain hanging around his neck of a dollar sign.

Afraid, Bodie tried to run until he heard the cock of their guns.

"So you went through all of this trouble to see me," Bodie said sitting in the chair across from the couch where Milli sat. "This ain't no dope house right?"

Milli shrugged. And in the cool manner he did everything else in life he responded. "You denied my last invitation for dinner, so I had to stage this elaborate show all for you."

"I'm surprised you here, because I heard about your situation at home."

Milli looked sad but he cleared his throat and squared off his shoulders. "I'm dealing with it," he responded firmly. "Let's leave it at that."

"So what do you want from me, man? Because I wasn't the one who wanted to rob you that day Ginger shot you and Gerron took the work," he lied. "That was all Gerron."

"That's neither here nor there. I'm here on other matters."

Bodie moved uneasily in his seat. "What matters
you want to discuss with me? Because I don't know
about nothing else."

"The streets are talking and they're saying you
have Milli's mother."

"Yeah...so?"

"So the streets also saying that in a few weeks you
meeting him for a big exchange. Some money for his
mother's life. Is that true?"

"I don't know what the fuck you talking 'bout."

Milli remained silent and Bodie could tell he
meant business even though Milli didn't say a word.
Bodie was certain that if he continued to play games he
would pay for it.

"Okay, I got her."

"Take me to her," Milli responded. "Now."

Milli and his men followed Bodie toward the entrance of an abandoned building. Milli's men made sure
their guns were still aimed on Bodie. They also had
more men outside of the building in case Bodie got slick.

As Milli walked down the steps, before he even
saw Gerron's mother, a stench was so strong in the air
it made Milli's stomach churn. When Milli walked down
the dark stairwell and bent the corner he smiled.
Gerron's mother was tied to a chair and she looked to

be in a bad state. Instead of feeling sorry for the woman who had been starved, and forced to sit in her own feces, he smiled and turned around to face Bodie.

"She's been here for a whole year?"

"Yeah," Bodie responded rubbing his arms. He needed some dope and he needed it bad. "I had some dudes feeding her while I was locked up, but they be forgetting sometimes and shit."

Milli looked at her again. "What's the longest she went without food?"

"About five days. Maybe more."

"Well I love what you have going on here," Milli responded nodding his head while looking at the dingy floors and ceiling. "A lot."

Bodie raised and eyebrow. "Why?"

"Because this will bring Gerron closer to us."

Bodie stepped back. "Fuck you mean closer to us? The money I'm getting from him is mine. All mine. I set this situation up not you."

Milli snapped his fingers and his men circled Bodie. "Listen, I already know you benefited from the nigga Gerron robbing me before he moved to Vegas. You don't have to lie because I know it's true. You sold some of the work Gerron stole from me to a close associate of mine. My product is branded and he knew the moment he got it where it came from."

Bodie widened his eyes.

"Now I need to get my hands on this nigga like yesterday. You can either help me or I can pull up an-

other chair next to his mother and put you in it. What's it gonna be?"

Bodie looked at Milli's men and realized he had no other choice. He was outnumbered. "Okay."

Milli smiled and patted his back. "Smart man."

"Are you mad 'cuz Gerron robbed you, or that he married Ginger?"

Milli's temples throbbed. He had no idea that they were married. He was an evil man who fucked Ginger over on a regular basis but in his mind he still had love for her, even if she shot him and ran off with Gerron. But to think that she dumped him and got up with a stick up nigga and married him made him look like a fool. He had to hit her hard, and he wanted to find the best way to do it.

"How do you know that?"

"Some dude name Hassan put the word out about him."

"I want you to start feeding her," Milli said. "Not just oatmeal and shit like that. But steaks, potatoes and rice."

Bodie shrugged. "Whatever."

"Whatever shit," Milli yelled. "I'm fucking serious."

"Aight, man. You got it."

Milli turned around to one of his men and said, "You still know that seamstress?"

"Yeah, she on that shit but she can still alter a mean suit."

"Good," he said with a devilish grin. "Call her for me. I need to see her ASAP."

"It's done."

CHAPTER 29

GINGER

Bodie and Milli stood next to the truck with grins on their faces. Another suburban that I couldn't see before was parked behind it.

"I wonder how these two mothafuckas got together," I said to Gerron.

He was silent.

I looked over at him. "Baby, what you thinking?"

"This is bad, real bad," he responded still looking at them, "but we don't have a choice. We gotta walk into the fire." He looked into my eyes. "They played their hands well. Too well."

"Damn, my daughter and your mother are over there...alive. And together."

Gerron's mother looked slim in the face, but at least she was alive. I knew for a fact why Milli brought Denise. He knew she was the one person who would make me step out of this car. He knew she was the one person who would make me come to him and I hated him for it.

"You ready?" he asked me rubbing my hair backwards. "Because you and I both know we are going to die today. That's something I can get behind."

Tears rolled down my face and I nodded. "At least it will be for love."

He pulled me to him and we kissed long, and passionately. When we were done I looked into his eyes. I saw tears in the wells but they weren't falling. He just stared at me, like he was looking into my soul for the last time.

"Our life together was short, baby, but it meant everything to me," he said. "I hope you can feel that."

I kissed him again and we gathered the money from the backseat.

"This is what we gonna do," Gerron said, "I'm gonna walk over there with the money and—"

"No, baby, I think I should walk over there."

"You sound crazy as shit. I'm not letting you walk over there and into their trap. You my wife now, Ginger."

"Listen to me," I said calmly. "I'm going to walk over there to make sure my baby and your mother are okay. You cover me by aiming at both of them with your guns."

"I can walk over there and do the same thing."

"No because they'll kill you and overpower me. This way I walk over and you can cover me. All four of us have a chance at surviving this way. So I will walk over there, you put the money over there near that bush. I'll tell Denise and your mother to step out of the truck. Then you drive toward me. Once we all back in the Civic, your mother and my daughter, then they can go get the paper."

"They not gonna go for it because they don't know how much money in the bags, baby. Them niggas is greedy not stupid."

"They don't have a choice. This is our plan and we make the rules. In our minds we gonna die anyway, so it's worth a try."

Gerron didn't seem to be buying it. "You right," he said softly. "Let's do it. But if you get a feeling that they about to do some slick shit come back to the car. I'd rather we go out blazing then by their hands."

"I got it, baby."

We eased out of the car and stood next to it. Gerron had two guns aimed at them and I walked to the front of the car and stopped at the hood. I sat on the rubber bumper and crossed my legs. Gerron was standing on the passenger side.

"Hello, Milli."

"Ginger," he said loudly. Although he only said one word I could feel the hate in his voice when he said it. "So I see you actually married the nigga next door huh? You don't have no standards do you?"

I shrugged. "What can I say? We found love so I said yes. Besides, he fucks better than you."

Gerron giggled. I figured he'd like that.

"Foul," he said spitting on the sand. "Real foul."

"Now let me ask you a question."

"Shoot," Milli responded.

Gerron cocked his guns. "Be careful with that word. My husband might take you seriously."

Milli was really angry now, I could tell by the way his forehead crinkled but I didn't give a fuck. "Why you bring our daughter here, Milli? Into all of this madness? What if something happens to her?"

"I brought her because she wanted to be with you, and I knew you wouldn't stop until she was back in your possession. I know you came to the house once when I wasn't there. Now you don't have to do that anymore. I brought her here to you."

I don't believe him. "Thank you."

"It's nothing."

"So this is how it's going to go down," Gerron interrupted. "She's going to come over there to check on our family. If they good I'm gonna walk the money over to that bush, then I'm gonna get in the car, pick them up and we gonna pull off.

"How do I know all the money is in that bag nigga?" Bodie asked.

I walked over to Gerron and unzipped one of the bags. Then I opened it sideways so that they could see that it was filled with stacks. I removed a few packs and went through the bills. When I was done I threw the stacks on the ground.

"You see, it's all money," I said to him. "And it's all there."

Milli grinned. "Okay, put the shit back in the bag and over there next to that bush like you said."

"Not until my wife makes sure our people are okay."

Milli smirked. "Whatever."

I walked over to Gerron, and while his arms were outstretched holding the guns, I walked in between them and kissed him. I looked into his eyes and said, "I love you, and it was a pleasure being your wife."

He looked over my shoulder at them and said, "And I feel the same way about being your husband. But it ain't over yet."

I took a deep breath and turned around to face Milli. If I thought he wanted to kill me at first now I felt like he wanted to carve me into a bunch of little pieces while I was still alive. It didn't bother me though. I wasn't going to risk walking over there without saying goodbye to Gerron in case I didn't make it.

Slowly I approached the car. The closer I got to the truck, and my smiling daughter I was hopeful that things would be okay. I was halfway over there when Gerron yelled.

"Stop right there, Ginger."

I obeyed. What happened? Did I miss something?

With guns stilled aimed he said, "Milli and Bodie, step away from the truck."

Surprisingly they didn't complain and they walked about twenty feet away.

"Go ahead, baby," Gerron continued.

I took another gulp of air and continued over to the car. When I reached the driver's side door, where Gerron's' mother sat behind the wheel, her expression seemed fake to me now. Unreal. I pulled the door open and when I did a strong odor hit me in the face. It smelled like rotten flesh. It wasn't until then that I could see that both my daughter and Gerron's' mother's faces were stitched at the corners of their mouths. To make their smiles stay in place.

I threw up on the side of the truck and it felt as if my insides were being ripped out.

Milli and Bodie ran to the truck behind us.

My daughter, my sweet baby girl, was dead and the fake smile was placed on her face to fool and hurt me. I was so caught up that I didn't see two niggas in the backseat until they were about to shoot me. I grabbed the weapon in my waist and fired three shots into the truck. The first went in the seat and over their heads but the other hit the left dude in the throat and the other in the head.

I turned around and faced Gerron. "It's a trap, baby," I yelled. "They are...my baby...is dead."

When I turned around Bodie and Milli were standing behind me. Gerron's expression turned from focused to evil and he gave me the look. I dropped to my knees and Gerron fired over my head at them. Everything seemed to be moving so fast.

I snatched Gerron's mother's corpse out of the truck and she plopped to the ground. Blood spilled from her body and I slipped on the step leading into the truck because there was so much blood coming out of her. When I hit the ground I heard a loud snap in my right shoulder and experienced the worst pain I ever imagined. I knew immediately my arm was broken or that my rotator cuff was torn.

Using my left arm, I hopped into the truck without looking at my daughter who was strapped in the passenger seat on my right. Like a doll. I closed the door with my good arm and tried to remain calm. But I couldn't. Her silhouette represented what I couldn't deal with now, that my daughter was dead and I didn't get a chance to say bye. I can't understand how Milli could kill his own child just to get at me. And I vowed that if I could make it out of this alive that he would pay for this shit.

As my husband fired at Milli and Bodie who were both shooting and approaching him, I rolled the window down and aimed at Milli but I shot Bodie instead when he caught my bullet to his head. I wanted Bodie dead but I knew who the real culprit was in this shit. It was Milli and because of it I wasn't satisfied. So I was trying to fire at him too but he was able to dip into the second suburban in the back.

I pressed on the gas and pulled the truck alongside Gerron. The moment he saw Denise his eyes widened and they were filled with so much sorrow. He could feel my pain I could tell.

He pulled the door open and looked at Denise. "Baby, I'm sorry."

"Pull her to the ground."

"But she's your daughter."

"PULL HER TO THE FUCKING GROUND! THAT AIN'T MY DAUGHTER! MY BABY'S DEAD!"

He did what I asked and I kept my eyes on the road ahead of us. I couldn't watch him do it but I knew what had to be done. Gerron pulled himself up trying to get into the truck when he caught a bullet to the chest. The t-shirt he was wearing immediately darkened with blood. He jumped inside anyway, slammed the door and looked over at me with wild eyes.

On the side of us was Kettle, Milli's uncle, who was driving. He wore a smile on his face. This nigga just shot my husband and he was grinning. Things were going out of control and I didn't know how to slow them down. My life was in complete shambles. Was this my Karma?

Before I could understand all of that, Kettle hopped out of the truck and was about to fire again. I steered to the right and ran over his body. I could feel the crunch of his flesh. When he was under the wheels I backed up and rolled over him again. I saw the look in Milli's eyes as his uncle met his fate.

"That's my girl," Gerron said in a weak voice.

"Be quiet, baby. You gotta preserve your energy."

"I know, but I...I gotta tell you something. I know you going to be mad at me but I had to do it."

"Now is not the time, Gerron. I gotta get you away to safety."

"It may be the only chance I get to tell you." He moaned a little and my heart broke inside but I had to be strong. I knew he was in pain. "I had a feeling shit was going to get crazy so I made a call."

I looked over to him. "To who?"

He didn't respond. His eyes were low and tears ran down my face. This was a living nightmare. Although our love is young, I still love him like we had been together all of my life and I couldn't imagine why this was happening.

I lost everything since I started fucking with Milli. First I lost my best friends who he fucked. Then I lost custody of Denise. Then I lost my daughter to death and now he was taking my husband too. I couldn't do it anymore. So I pressed my foot on the gas and ran Kettle over again. I had killed his uncle and Milli felt it on all levels of his soul. I could feel it.

I knew I had to get out of here now to get myself and my husband to safety. So I pressed the gas and took off. I was driving about ninety miles per hour. I never realized it before, but at that moment I felt guilty. Had I not convinced Gerron to take me with him the day we first got together, he wouldn't be involved in any of this and his mother would still be alive.

I tried not to think about it until Milli's truck pulled up on the right and he sent more bullets into the car. He was mad and hurt but so was I. What about my daughter? And now my husband? Fuck him and his feelings!

When I smelled the scent of gasoline I knew somebody hit the gas tank.

"My mama wasn't alive?" Gerron asked in a lower voice.

I shook my head no.

"I'm sorry, baby. They took both of them."

I didn't look at him, but I could tell that he was crying. He was probably overwhelmed with grief. God please help us. Please help me help my husband. I lost my daughter; don't take him away from me too.

After saying my prayer when I looked over at him he was staring at me. His eyes were open but I couldn't tell if he was with me anymore because he was stiff. If he was still in this world. His t-shirt now had a big circle of blood on it from where he was shot.

"I'm gonna get you out of here, Gerron," I said looking at him and then back at the road. "Just don't fucking die on me. I can't be—"

My thought was broken when a hot slug crashed into the back window of the truck, and tore into the flesh of my left hand. I could tell that Milli wanted me dead and he was willing to do anything to see it happen.

"Leave me alone," I screamed looking at the truck in my rearview mirror. I was beyond overwhelmed. "Just leave us alone!"

Although my only functional hand was now injured I did all I could to maintain control of the SUV. But when another bullet ripped into the flesh of my only good arm I was done. All of the fighting, everything I did to keep us alive was all in vain. I lost my daughter and my husband, and it was now okay that I died too.

Since I could no longer drive I tried to steer the truck with my knee. That shit didn't work. I couldn't control the gas and wheel and we were now going fifty miles an hour toward a silver tractor-trailer that was parked on the side of the road.

As I watched Milli's sly smile in the rearview mirror, I slammed into the trailer so hard my head hit the steering wheel and then flew back into the driver's seat.

Milli sped away leaving me for dead.

CHAPTER 30

AFTER DEATH

Ginger got out of the truck and looked at the wreckage. Her breath felt trapped inside of her throat. She survived the mess. Until she realized she was looking at herself still bloodied and penned inside of the driver seat. But how could that be possible? Slowly she walked toward the driver's side window and glanced over at the passenger seat. She also saw Gerron's body and his eyes were still open and staring out into space. She was about to run toward his side of the truck until she heard his voice. The two bodies she killed earlier were also inside the backseat.

"Baby, I'm over here."

Ginger stopped in place and turned around. She was staring at her husband who was standing outside of the truck smiling at her. She glanced inside of the truck again and he was there too. What was going on?

"Baby, I'm scared?" She walked toward him. "What's happening?"

He smiled. "It's over, Ginger. We don't have to deal with anymore pain."

"I'm still not understanding."

"We're dead."

She covered her mouth. "But I don't want to...I mean..."

"It's okay, Ginger. Your daughter is here, my mother is here and it's serenity. I feel like everything we fought for was all for nothing. Here we will be in extreme peace for eternity." He extended his hand. "Come with me."

Ginger shook her head no and stepped back. "I'm not ready to die! Do you hear me? I don't want to fucking die. I have so much to do. So much to live for. I need my fucking revenge!"

The smile washed off of his face. "Then what do you want to do? Stay in a world that's full of hate, and strife? When we have a chance to rest in peace? Forever? Baby, I don't want to go back. I want to be here with my mother, your daughter and you."

"Milli took everything from me, Gerron! Every fucking thing and I want him to pay for it. I want my revenge. If I'm in heaven, then he better be in hell mad about it."

"Ginger, if you leave this place on some revenge shit, when you finally die you will never rest in peace. Your soul will be condemned forever. Is that what you want?"

"For a chance to get back at him—yes."

Gerron's head hung low as he looked at the ground. He took a deep breath and then looked at her again. "Then I'm going with you."

EPILOGUE

Ginger's eyes popped open as the truck she was driving rested in the side of the tractor trailer as if it were suppose to be there. Smoke and gas was everywhere and she couldn't believe she actually survived. When she looked to her right, Gerron's eyes were moving but it appeared that he couldn't move his body.

When Ginger's head moved to the left, and she looked out of the window she was staring at a familiar face. But what was she doing there? It was Ric, the woman who she and Gerron robbed. It was also the chick who Gerron fucked while Ginger slept with her husband.

Ric was covered by three more men and they all looked at the wreckage with amazement in their eyes. It was at that time that Ginger remembered what Gerron said in the truck earlier. He said she was going to be mad but he made a call, and now she understood what he meant. Gerron always said the rich stayed bored maybe that was why Ric was there.

"Gerron called me earlier and said you needed help. Don't worry," she grinned. "Mama's got you now."

THE CARTEL PUBLICATIONS

PRESENTS

THE
UNGRATEFUL
BASTARDS

T. STYLES

NATIONAL BESTSELLING AUTHOR OF *RAUNCHY*

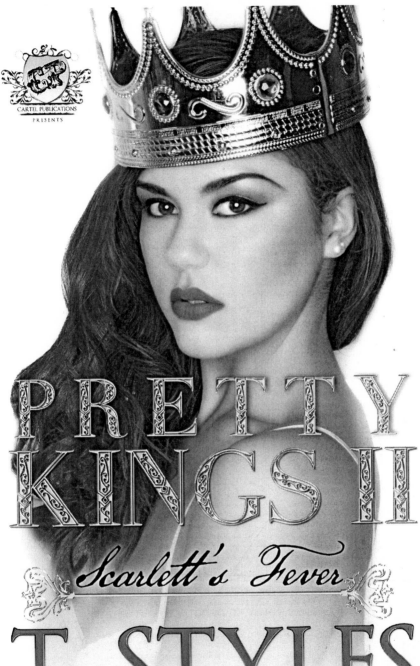

CARTEL PUBLICATIONS
PRESENTS

The Cartel Collection
Established in January 2008
We're growing stronger by the month!!!
www.thecartelpublications.com

Cartel Publications Order Form
Inmates <u>ONLY</u> get novels for $10.00 per book!

<u>Titles</u>	<u>Fee</u>
Shyt List	$15.00
Shyt List 2	$15.00
Pitbulls In A Skirt	$15.00
Pitbulls In A Skirt 2	$15.00
Pitbulls In A Skirt 3	$15.00
Pitbulls In A Skirt 4	$15.00
Victoria's Secret	$15.00
Poison	$15.00
Poison 2	$15.00
Hell Razor Honeys	$15.00
Hell Razor Honeys 2	$15.00
A Hustler's Son 2	$15.00
Black And Ugly As Ever	$15.00
Year of The Crack Mom	$15.00
The Face That Launched a Thousand Bullets	
	$15.00
The Unusual Suspects	$15.00
Miss Wayne & The Queens of DC	
	$15.00
Year of The Crack Mom	$15.00
Paid in Blood	$15.00
Shyt List III	$15.00
Shyt List IV	$15.00
Raunchy	$15.00
Raunchy 2	$15.00
Raunchy 3	$15.00
Jealous Hearted	$15.00
Quita's Dayscare Center	$15.00
Quita's Dayscare Center 2	$15.00
Shyt List V	$15.00
Deadheads	$15.00
Pretty Kings	$15.00
Drunk & Hot Girls	$15.00
Hersband Material	$15.00
Upscale Kittens	$15.00
Wake & Bake Boys	$15.00
Young & Dumb	$15.00
Tranny 911	$15.00
First Comes Love Then Comes Murder	$15.00
Young & Dumb: Vyce's Getback	$15.00
Luxury Tax	$15.00

Please add $4.00 per book for shipping and handling.
The Cartel Publications * P.O. Box 486 * Owings Mills * MD * 21117

Name: _____

Address: _____

City/State: _____

Contact # & Email: _____

Please allow 5-7 business days for delivery. The Cartel is not responsible for prison orders rejected.

<u>*Personal Checks Are Not Accepted.*</u>